OUTSIDE

DAVID BRUNICARDI

LANDS

Wasteland Press

www.wastelandpress.net
Shelbyville, KY USA

Outside Lands
by David Brunicardi

Copyright © 2013 David Brunicardi
ALL RIGHTS RESERVED

First Printing—June 2013
ISBN: 978-1-60047-872-7
Author photograph © Nathalie Wolf

Library of Congress Cataloging-in-Publication Data
Brunicardi, David
Outside Lands / David Brunicardi
p. cm.
Contents: Terrarium—Seeds of Antipathy—Mountainous—Drawbridge—
The Quickening Of Ethan Boyd—Wawona—The Absconding Sea
ISBN
1. West Coast (U.S.)—Fiction. I. Title

Printed in the U.S.A.

0   1   2   3   4   5

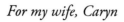

For my wife, Caryn

CONTENTS

TERRARIUM

They sat around the campfire laughing, save Elizabeth, who felt a little too raw to join in the revelry. She sat silently staring into the fire, holding a tin cup of strong coffee between her hands. A morning dew had settled upon the forest, softening the edges, polishing their camp with an unnatural sheen. Her fiancé Scott sat down next to her on the damp log.

"What's up, Liz? You didn't drink that much last night," he said.

She stared into the fire a moment longer, searching for an answer, for the reason behind her malaise. "Yeah, I know, that's what's so weird. I feel like I got hit by a truck. I mean even my arms and legs hurt … that's no hangover." She pushed her dark hair from her eyes. "I guess I'm just achy from sleeping with only a half inch of foam between me and the cold earth."

She looked up from the fire. Her friends, Katie and Aaron, who were sitting across from her, seemed to share none of her discomfort. She turned back to Scott and wondered if he could read her worry.

"You must really be hurting, because that doesn't sound like you at all, the original happy camper," he said. "Anyway, we have three more nights to go, you gonna make it?"

"You know I am. This trip was my idea, remember?"

She turned to look at him. Elizabeth could see that he was studying her face and it made her uncomfortable. "What?" she said.

"Nothing," said Scott, adjusting his baseball cap. "Something about the morning light I guess."

She was about to ask him what he meant by that when on the opposite side of the fire Aaron stood up, holding his battered coffee cup out as if he were going to make a toast. "Oye, compadres. Anyone besides me want some tequila in their morning cup of joe?" he asked.

Katie, sitting next to him, laughed and gave Aaron a flirty look. She flipped her strawberry blond hair back and cocked her head in his direction. "Why not?" she said, raising her cup.

"Extraordinary. I second that motion my good man," replied Scott, trying to sound like a British aristocrat. "Got to be better than that bloody gin you dispensed last night." He stood up to join his friends on the other side of the fire.

All eyes turned to Elizabeth, who hadn't moved her gaze from the hypnotic fire. "Third," she said, without looking up. Her voice didn't carry the same enthusiasm as it had the previous evening and she hoped that the hot coffee and a little 'hair of the dog' would ease the pain that had arrived sometime in the night.

The improvised Mexican coffee seemed to be hitting the spot and Elizabeth joined in the reminiscing already underway around the morning fire. A swirling mist clung to the hilltops that surrounded their encampment and shrouded the top of the tree line. The clearing where they made camp last night had been given a reprieve and revealed itself to be a beautiful meadow.

"Wow, look at this place," said Katie. The field, even under overcast skies, was ablaze with California poppies, their fiery orange flowers a perfect contrast to the surrounding ancient oaks that marched their way up the hills until they disappeared into the white.

The four friends gazed respectfully at the serene beauty. Suddenly, the skies echoed with a loud thundering moan. The sound was immense, like huge pieces of steel twisting under enormous pressure. The ground shook below their feet as the sound reverberated between the hills. It lasted about five seconds and then fell silent. A small flock of frightened birds took to the sky. They disappeared into the fog and then fell lifelessly back into the trees, like stones.

Elizabeth grabbed Scott's arm. "What the hell was that?" she said.

They were frantically looking around in all directions, searching for any possible source of the noise.

"Must've been a falling tree," said Aaron, rubbing his hand across his close-cropped hair.

"Yeah, that's what I was thinking too," said Scott.

"Are you kidding? That was no tree. It sounded metallic to me," replied Elizabeth. "Huge, scary, metal."

"Yeah, but there's nothing like that out here. This is the wilderness," said Scott.

"Airplane maybe?" said Aaron.

"Did anyone hear a crash?" asked Elizabeth. "I mean, it didn't sound like an explosion, right?" She already knew the answer. After looking at the face of each of her friends she uttered the answer, "No."

"It was more of a wrenching sound," said Scott with apprehension.

Katie was still looking around and up to the sky. "Why did the birds fall from the sky?" she asked softly.

Elizabeth wondered the same thing. She stared at Katie for a moment, answerless. Scott broke the silence and said, "Hey, we should pack up and move on. Maybe we'll figure out what that sound was along the way. We're still trying to make it to Ohlone Lake right?"

"Dude, you know it," said Aaron, attempting levity. "No swimsuits, right girls?"

Elizabeth forced a laugh along with the others and they began breaking camp. She noticed they were all looking over their shoulders every chance they got.

They had been walking for a few hours and Elizabeth was aching from head to toe. Everyone was still arguing about the source of the ominous sound and theories were being shot down almost as soon as they were offered. The absence of any visual clues left them stabbing in the dark.

"Can we talk about something else?" said Elizabeth, in a tone that was uncharacteristically brusque. An awkward silence spread among the friends as they trudged deeper into the woods.

"Maybe we should break for lunch soon?" asked Scott.

Aaron nodded appreciatively. His pack was heavier than the others because he was carrying most of the liquor, a self-imposed responsibility. The hilly terrain only added to his woes. He swung his backpack off of his shoulders and let it rest on the dirt trail while he looked at a map. "I'm not certain, because I suck at reading maps, but it looks like there is a campsite just under a mile to the east, Bottcher's Gap. Sounds perfect for us. I'd say were pretty good at botching things up." Aaron smiled broadly. "Let's set up camp there and start the party early."

"I'm in," said Katie, without hesitation.

Elizabeth looked at Scott. Normally she would have argued to keep pressing on, but she really wanted to rest. Her eyes must have conveyed the message for her because Scott just shook his head in agreement at the sight of her. She realized that they were all still a little unnerved by the mysterious earth shaking sound.

"Alright," said Aaron. "Let's do this." He opened a Red Bull, poured a little something into it and bounded off down the trail like a puppy out for a walk.

"Kids these days," said Scott, shaking his head.

They fell in behind Aaron and started heading east. The persistent fog continued to surround the oaks and madrones as they headed down the narrow trail. Condensation had collected upon the leaves that covered the path, making it slippery and they each took a turn landing on their backsides, laughing.

Scott turned to Elizabeth and said, "Mind if I talk with Aaron for bit?" She gave him a tender smile and shook her head yes. He jogged ahead to catch up to his old high school buddy who was blazing down the trail whistling old TV jingles. Katie fell in alongside Elizabeth and the two friends had a moment alone.

"Geez, what's with this fog?" said Katie.

"I wish I knew. It's really weird. It almost has a luminescent quality, don't you think?"

"I hadn't really thought about it but, yeah, you're right. Must be the sun trying to burn through."

"It should thin out as we keep moving further from the coast," said Elizabeth.

The path took them into a grove of redwoods. Conifer needles covered the ground and every sound was dampened by the preponderance of furry bark that covered the majestic trees. They were enjoying the silence, quite content with just the sound of their own breathing.

Elizabeth and Katie were roommates in college their freshman year. Elizabeth was grateful that their friendship didn't require small talk to fill in the silence. From the corner of her eye she could see that Katie was glancing at her face, making her wonder if Scott did see something earlier, something that made her look different. What she did know for certain was that every part of her body ached, no reminder needed. She gave Katie an inquisitive look and her friend, realizing she had been discovered, quickly started a conversation.

"So, have you guys set a date yet?" she asked.

"No, Scott wants to finish his MBA. We're thinking sometime next summer," replied Elizabeth, her gait becoming more labored. "You and Aaron seem to be hitting it off."

"You think so? That's good to hear. I do like him a lot," said Katie. She tucked a wayward strand of hair behind her ear and gave Elizabeth a sideways glance. "Would love some behind the scenes information from Scott, but I'm too embarrassed to ask."

"You should just ask him. He's known the guy a lot longer than me." Elizabeth pointed to a tiny trail sign that read Bottcher's Gap. "Oh, hey, I think we're here," she said.

The fern-lined trail dead ended near a stream. Aaron turned at the sound of their approach. "Ta da," he said as he held his arms up. The primitive campsite was a circle of fallen trees around a ring of blackened stones that housed the charred remains of a hundred campfires.

The women took off their packs and leaned them against a log. Katie walked over to where Aaron was setting up his tent and started to help. Elizabeth could see Scott was standing at the edge of the stream a few yards off. "You catching our trout lunch?" she shouted.

"I wish," he said. "Come check this out." He waved her over. As she headed in his direction she could see that they had arrived in a beautiful little glen with moss-covered rocks set amongst redwoods and ferns. The mist leant it a surreal, fairytale-like quality.

"So peaceful," she said, joining him by the edge of the creek.

"Yeah, but it's weird." Scott pointed to the water. "This is a pretty big creek, big enough to be on the map. And yet it isn't moving. Look at the water, it's still. There are no fish that I've seen ... not even a single water spider."

"Maybe it was a dry year?" she said.

"They get pretty much the same weather here that we do in San Francisco. We had a very wet year," he said. "And it's not just that. Have you seen any more birds, or a squirrel, or even a fly for that matter?"

Elizabeth wanted to find an answer, but none came. "I don't know, babe. I'm the wrong person to ask. From the way I feel, to that noise this morning, to the way you are all looking at me, I don't know anymore." She felt tired and wondered if her eyes conveyed the same resignation that had begun to choke off her will. She let out a sigh and said, "Want to set up camp and eat some lunch? I'm starving."

"Yeah, me too." Scott took one last look at the unmoving water. "Me too."

The campfire crackled and snapped in the silent forest, the smoke braiding itself into the fog that swirled around the trees. Elizabeth and Scott had just said goodnight and were in their tent setting up for bed. She could hear Katie and Aaron sitting alone by the glowing fire, quietly laughing and talking. They had all had too much to drink again and had spent the evening trying to embarrass each other with stories from college and childhood.

From within the tent Elizabeth and Scott could see the silhouettes of their friends sitting shoulder to shoulder on the log near the fire. "They're cute aren't they?" Elizabeth mumbled.

Scott, sitting on the floor, smiled in her direction and said in a quiet voice, "He really likes her."

Elizabeth began taking off her flannel shirt and jeans. She was aware of her fiancé watching her as she pulled on her merino thermal underwear. She hoped that she looked like the same woman that he had fallen in love with, that the dim tent light would not reveal whatever subtle differences her friends saw today. From her periphery she could see him rise from the floor and move in behind her, kissing her neck. She felt his hands slide to her hips and she turned to meet his lips.

They kissed their way to the floor until they found their way into one of the sleeping bags. Any remnant of anxiety melted away and they made love, the only sound their own breathing and the subtle chime of the sleeping bag zipper.

Afterward they lay entwined, satisfied, and reassured. Scott whispered in Elizabeth's ear, "I'll be right back." She watched him shimmy his way out of the bag and throw on his faded blue jeans.

"What are you doing?" she said, watching him unzip their tent and peek his head out. He didn't acknowledge her but she assumed he was making sure that Katie and Aaron were no longer by the fire. He tip-toed outside.

Elizabeth, in a languid daze, could hear him rustling around breaking little twigs. After a few minutes he came back inside the tent holding a bundle of sticks whose ends had been charred in the fire and then wet down. Elizabeth smiled and let out a little laugh. She rolled onto her stomach with her hands folded out in front of her.

When they first went camping years ago Scott had used burnt sticks to make temporary drawings on her back and arms, much like henna tattoos. Scott, who had always dabbled in art, would draw simple line drawings of plants and animals upon her slender torso.

She could feel the caress of the tiny twigs as he drew delicately upon her skin, their movement eliciting goose bumps along the way. The charcoal rendering depicted two doves sitting on the branch of a delicate maple tree. The light from the fire began to fade and Elizabeth was falling into a trancelike state, on the threshold of sleep. In a whisper she said, "Let's go to bed." She lazily pulled her thermal top back on and settled into her soft down bag. She could hear Scott fumbling around in the dark, setting up his own sleeping bag next to hers. Outside was complete silence.

Elizabeth was the last to rise. Her headache had returned and it was even more severe than the day before. She felt a little nauseas and it seemed to take awhile for her to remember where she was. She felt like she was a hundred years old as she tried to get out of her sleeping bag. Once she was on her feet she let out a groan and had to grab onto a tent pole to not fall back down.

"You all right in there, Lizzie?" came Katie's voice.

Elizabeth started looking for her hooded sweatshirt and some pants to pull on over her long underwear. "Uh, yeah. I think so. Not feeling too good though," she said in a pained voice. "I'll be right out, Katie."

"Ok. We're all a little hung over again I'm afraid," said Katie. "The boys are just down at the stream, washing some of our gear."

Elizabeth fell over while putting her pants on so she decided to finish dressing while lying on the ground. When she had her pants on she crawled to the front of the tent and pulled up the zipper to the flap. She emerged into the bright fog with one hand over her forehead, shielding her eyes.

"Good morni ...." Katie started to say as she turned to meet Elizabeth, dropping the cup she had ready for her friend. "Oh my God," she said, recoiling slightly. "What happened, Liz?"

Elizabeth brought her hand from her eyes and Katie let out a little scream. She was staring at Elizabeth's face with open repulsion.

"Aaron! Scott!" Katie called. "Come quick!"

Scott bounded up from the creek toward the two women. He drew in a sharp breath as he reached Elizabeth and stopped abruptly. Elizabeth stared at him, trying to read the face of the man who knew her so well. His expression filled her with horror. She knew that something was terribly wrong. Aaron who had just come up from the creek fell in beside Katie. "Holy shit," he said. "Elizabeth?"

They stood in front of her with their mouths agape, not knowing what to do.

"What? What is it?" she screamed. Nobody moved or said a word. Elizabeth's desperation overwhelmed her and she broke down crying.

She looked up at Scott and could almost see the abject fear pouring into him. He put his arms around her and tried to console her. "I'm sorry, baby. You'll be ok. I think you're just sick, that's all."

She broke free of his grasp, "I need to see myself" she said. "Do any of you have a mirror?" She was sobbing and grabbed onto Scott with one arm to steady herself. Katie and Aaron started looking through their packs and around the camp for anything shiny. Aaron emerged with a chrome thermos top.

"Liz, try this," he said, handing it to her.

Elizabeth held the small disc up to her face, gazed silently, and dropped it to the dirt. She wasn't sure whom, or what, she had seen. All familiarity, all self-recognition, had vanished overnight. She didn't even recognize her eyes. It was as though she had been in an accident years ago and a team of surgeons attempted to rebuild her face.

She held her head to the sky and screamed. She screamed until her lungs were empty and then opened her eyes. While she was looking up she thought she saw a tiny patch of fog open up revealing not blue, but black. She lowered her head and in a calm voice said, "We have to get out of here."

Scott said, "I agree, we need to get you to a hospital." He looked back to Katie and Aaron and they nodded in approval.

"No, you don't understand," said Elizabeth. "There is something wrong with this place. We are all in danger here."

Scott could not conceal his worry, nor could Katie or Aaron. Elizabeth could see that there was no doubt in their minds that she had fallen victim to something they could not yet comprehend.

"Just pack what you need for the day," said Scott. "We're not stopping until we get to the car."

Elizabeth was already trying to pack up her things. The hood from her hooded sweatshirt hung down low as she stooped over to snatch up the gear she deemed necessary. Scott was standing directly behind her. She could sense that he was staring at her and it made her uncomfortable. "What are you doing?" she said, turning her stiff neck until she could see him.

"Oh. Sorry. I was looking at the drawing I did last night."

She saw him frown and move in closer. "Hold still for a minute, babe," he said. She paused while he held her by the shoulders and studied the delicate tree branches he had drawn on her back the night before. "It's really weird," he said. "It's as though every line in the drawing has been severed and reattached, the alignment off by a fraction of an inch."

"What are you saying? That I've been cut apart and put back together?"

Scott laughed nervously. "No. That would be impossible. I think it must have been the way you slept in your bag last night. It just rubbed parts of the drawing off, that's all."

Elizabeth righted herself but remained on her knees, like a fighter, swaying, refusing to go down. She stared into space for a moment and then resumed packing. "We have to leave," she said. "Now."

She felt sick to her stomach. Could it be that she had somehow been dissected and then miraculously reattached without any recollection of it happening? Without any scars? This was more than she could process. All that mattered was getting out of the forest as fast as possible.

Scott knelt next to her at the mouth of the tent and started shoveling things into his bag. "How's everybody doing?" he said. She could hear a greater sense of urgency in his voice now.

"Almost ready," replied Aaron from the other side of the camp. "I'm leaving a ton of stuff behind though."

"Me too," said Katie, not looking up from the pile of gear she was sorting through on the ground.

Soon they all had their lean packs ready, including Elizabeth. They helped her to her feet and she said, "Let's get the hell out of here." They started up the trail and after a few minutes it was clear that Elizabeth could not keep up with the anxious pace that the group adopted. Scott was hanging back at her side but Katie and Aaron were already several yards ahead.

"Hey, you guys. Wait up," Scott shouted.

Katie and Aaron stopped until Scott and Elizabeth could catch up. The fog was so thick that Elizabeth could barely discern them from the grove of redwoods that surrounded the trail. The group huddled on the inclining trail and Elizabeth rested against the soft trunk of a tree. Everyone was breathing heavily but she was near the point of collapse. Yet she did not complain and was hesitant to stop at all.

"I think we need to modify our plan," said Scott.

"What are you thinking, man? replied Aaron.

"I'm thinking you and Katie should plow ahead as fast as you can. If you're up for running, even better. Here are the keys to the Jeep. Do whatever you have to do to get that thing down the trail and pick up me and Liz, ok? Just stay on the same trail because we'll be following it back. All right?"

"Yeah. We're on it," Aaron said.

Katie walked up to Elizabeth and gave her a hug. "It's going to be ok, Lizzie. We're going to get you to a doctor. We promise." Elizabeth didn't reply, she was too busy trying to catch her breath. She squeezed her friend tight and wheezed in her ear, "Don't stop."

Katie joined Aaron and the two began to jog ahead, quickly disappearing into the mist. Scott put Elizabeth's arm around his shoulder and they began climbing the trail together. Elizabeth summoned a latent strength to keep herself moving forward. She held on to Scott tightly and her mind raced. Something was very wrong with where they were and she was afraid of the moment when she would find out what.

Scott started talking about their wedding plans and ideas for their honeymoon. She knew he was trying to keep her distracted, and she welcomed the effort. The fog surrounding them had become so heavy it was like a light rain now. The moisture made the trail slick and they slogged onward through the trees.

Elizabeth and Scott had been hiking for hours and she relied on him to take more and more of her weight with each mile. Finally they emerged from the canopy of redwoods. She knew that they were roughly halfway to the entrance of the park where they had parked their car. "We have to hurry," she said between breaths. "We need to get out of here before dark. I won't spend another night here." They trudged through the oak-dotted foothills in the rain, their wet clothes clinging to their bodies.

"Do you think that Aaron and Katie have reached the car yet?" asked Elizabeth.

"I don't think so. Even if they ran most of the way they still probably have two hours ahead of them, and none of us are in top form now."

"What?" she said in a weak voice. "Oh, yeah, I know. But they're motivated, Scott. They don't want to wind up like me."

"That's not true. You know they're not thinking like that," he said. "We don't even know what's up with you yet. You could be having an allergic reaction or something."

"I'm putting my money on 'or something'," she said.

She made a sound just shy of a laugh and it helped thin out the fear, momentarily.

"I just hope they find a way to get the Jeep onto the trail. If the rain keeps up and it gets dark, we may need to stop …."

"No," she interrupted. "No stopping."

Elizabeth and Scott moved like they were one, his right hand clutching her arm around his shoulder and his left holding her at the waist. Their legs were locked in a limping gait that resembled a lame animal. They plodded along with cold feet, stoically traversing the slippery path.

Further along they saw something sitting in the middle of trail. They thought it may just be a large rock but as they got closer, they could see that it was Katie's backpack. "Oh no," said Elizabeth. She knelt down in front of the wet pack. "No, no, no."

Scott darted between the oaks and laurels surrounding the trail and called Katie's name. After a couple of minutes of searching he rejoined Elizabeth on trail. She was holding Katie's bag by one of the straps as if she were about to pick it up.

"Maybe she and Aaron decided they only needed one bag," he said.

Elizabeth was crying and shook her head no. "Come look at this," she said with renewed fright. "The pack is frozen where it touches the earth. Like the cold is coming from the ground, not from the sky." She peeled the bag off the moist dirt and showed Scott the white frost that had formed on its underside.

"We have to keep moving," he said.

They stumbled along the muddy trail, and Scott shouted for their friends in every direction. The rain and her limp caused them to move slower than they wanted. They could see the remnants of foot and handprints on the muddy trail, as though someone had been clawing their way forward.

About a hundred yards ahead they found Aaron's backpack. An indescribable cold crawled into Elizabeth that she recognized as hopelessness. Scott left her on the trail while he ran into the underbrush frantically calling for Katie and Aaron. Elizabeth could hear his apprehensive voice rise above the rain, the sharp snap of branches breaking as he tore through the brush. Then, without warning, his shouting inexplicably stopped, severed mid-word. There was nothing but thick silence.

"Scott?" called Elizabeth. She repeated his name several times with increasing despair. Nothing. She brought her hand to her face and was reminded of its unfamiliarity. She limped between the trees, stepping into the muddy footprints of her fiancé. The ground was uneven and wet and she almost slid down the slope that arced from the trail. She was screaming Scott's name now, raw primal screams that went unanswered.

As the copse of trees began to thin she could see that Scott's footprints just stopped, no sign of struggle, no sign of him. She surveyed the landscape in all directions, the only movement came from leaves undulating in the uniform rain.

The sky had dimmed to a dark gray but she knew it had to be early afternoon. The compulsion to run seized control of her. The gradual hill provided her broken stride with much needed momentum, and she was almost running. She didn't know to where, but she wasn't going to stop.

The exertion was painful and Elizabeth began to hyperventilate, growing more lightheaded by the minute. "Where are you?" she screamed to everyone and no one. She almost didn't recognize her voice, which had become a rudimentary growl, like that of a cornered animal. Her feet were carrying her blindly down the hill. Suddenly she collided with something full force. The impact sent her sailing backwards and she fell onto the wet groundcover below. She lay there for a minute, bewildered by what just happened. She thought that the closest tree was five feet away yet she hit something hard.

The blow had split her lip. Blood was trickling into her mouth, and she could taste the iron on her tongue.

She forced herself up and stepped with trepidation toward the point where she had slammed into the unknown. As she drew nearer, the area between the trees seemed to be black, like what she had witnessed earlier when the fog momentarily parted. Elizabeth held out an arm as she inched forward, and a chill ran down her spine as she touched something hard and flat, invisible. It didn't feel like glass, but it was definitely a wall. Standing directly in front of it she could see that every tree to her right and left had been cut vertically along the same invisible line. Some were cut in half, some only missing their branches on one side, but each had been cut like they were mere decorations on a slice of birthday cake. She looked down and felt faint as she discovered that the earth had also been incised along the same line. Rocks, roots and soil cleaved along the same boundary.

Elizabeth moved her face to the invisible barrier and let out a sorrowful bellow. On the other side lay only the vast expanse of space. An infinite blackness pierced by innumerable unwarming stars. She gazed hypnotically into the void, arrested by its indifferent emptiness. As she turned to once again run, a newfound longing entered her heart. Not for any individual, but for home.

THE SEEDS OF ANTIPATHY

Blake hurried in from the cold through the back door off the deck on the second floor. He balanced a quartet of coffee in his left hand, the corrugated cardboard tray wet from his shaky ascent. It was still two hours till dawn so he kept his footsteps light, not wanting to wake anyone. The terrace door opened into the upstairs bath and he was immediately comforted by the smell of soap and his wife, pretty things, optimistic things.

He set the tray down on the vanity and took out one of the steaming cups of coffee. The pungent aroma of the French Roast overwhelmed the soft scent of bath soap, pinning it to the ground. Blake didn't need to be at the airport for another two hours so he sat down on the edge of the tub and began to consume the near scalding liquid. When he finished the first cup he moved on to the second, and then the third. He saved the fourth for his sleeping wife, Michelle. He figured he hadn't slept more than two or three hours in the past two days.

Neither Blake nor Michelle had fully recovered from the shock of their son, Evan, nearly drowning three days prior. It was a Friday afternoon, the first sunny day after a week of rain, and everyone had been suffering from cabin fever. Evan was playing with his trucks in the backyard, making engine sounds and prattling to himself. Blake and Michelle were preparing an early dinner, keeping one eye on him through the kitchen window that sat above the sink.

A forgotten wheelbarrow, tucked tightly against the house just under the kitchen window, had filled to the brim with rainwater. It was a heavy duty barrow, deep and sturdy. When Michelle returned to the sink to drain the pasta into the colander she saw her son's muddy feet kicking in the air while he and his favorite truck lay submerged in the dark, rusty water.

Her legs were already in motion as the pot fell from her hands, her dreadful scream pulling Blake behind her. By the time they ran outside and rounded the corner Evan was no longer moving. Blake stopped short of the wheelbarrow, as though an unseen hand was holding him back, "Oh, shit. Oh, shit," he repeated in a panicked falsetto voice. He just stood there, paralyzed. A crippling fear had invaded his otherwise swift mind.

Michelle grabbed the boy by his legs and pulled him from the murky water. He swung upside down as if he was hanging from a trapeze as she screamed his name. She carried him to the driveway and turned to look at her husband. "What are you doing?" she demanded. "Help him." Not once in their five years together had she seen Blake unable to respond to a situation. "Don't just stand there," she shouted. "Call 911." Yet, there he stood, his mouth aquiver, breathlessly attempting to form words. A confluence of tears and rainwater met on the asphalt as she cradled her limp son in her arms.

"Damn it, I don't know what to do," she screamed.

Suddenly Blake snapped to attention, as if waking from a dream. He ran to her side. "I'll start CPR, you call 911," he said.

"Are you sure you can handle this? Are you with us?"

"Yes. I'm sorry. Go, call an ambulance."

She handed him their son and ran toward the door to make the call. She stopped briefly to look back, making sure that her husband was still lucid before she stepped inside. Blake, recalling a CPR course he had taken years before, lay Evan on his side, striking him on the back between the shoulder blades. Each blow made a sickening thud that tested Blake's resolve. He stuck a finger into the boy's mouth and cleared out some silt and a couple of wet leaves. He let him roll back onto his back. The sight of his drowned son, peacefully lying in the driveway like a wet doll, caused him to shudder. In a strangled whisper, Blake squeezed out the word "No." He tilted the boy's head backward and pinched his tiny nose closed. He breathed gently into him, wishing he could sacrifice his breath for his son's. He was about to start chest compressions when suddenly Evan coughed up water and began to cry.

Blake began to cry along with him as he was joined by his wife, the sound of the dispatcher's voice still emanating from the cordless phone in her hand. They held their boy between them, and Blake shivered as something he had buried within himself clawed its way into his consciousness, no longer willing to remain hidden.

Blake took a couple of sleeping pills as he waited in the boarding area at the Portland airport. Escaping time, even for a few hours, was imperative. He didn't want to be alone with his head any longer, especially in the suffocating environment of an overcrowded aluminum tube. He boarded the plane and found his seat, then sank back into the worn fabric, welcoming the creeping inertia that spread through him. He began to doze and was immediately awakened by the gliss of a pearly clarinet as the airline's adopted theme song was piped into the cabin.

It was as though some omniscient force was determined to exhume what lay beneath, allowing it to tunnel up through the deep recesses of his collected past. The interior of the plane began to fade away and a dark vision invaded his mind. He saw only a vast, black pool of water, above which a single drop fell from an unseen ceiling, creating concentric rings that spread silently beyond an almost imperceptible object bobbing on the surface. A clarinet case. Edward Kovacs' clarinet case.

Blake began to panic. He unbuckled his seat belt and stood up. He was immediately met by a collection of frowns from the other passengers nearby. The jet was still taxiing down the runway and he wanted to make a run for the cabin door, jump onto the tarmac and keep on running. He thought about the consequences and instead sat back down. He leaned forward and pressed the palms of his hands against his face until the vision faded. A stream of buried memories began to bubble up to the surface, perforating the protective mantle he had developed over the years.

When he was a boy Blake would walk home from school with the same two friends, Luke Dalton and Ronald Petrosian. Occasionally they would be joined by a random friend or acquaintance who would also be making the trek. Together the nine year olds would scale the bleak, concrete-covered dunes that comprised the Sunset District, San Francisco's suburb within the city. One by one they would peel off down their own treeless block, passing row after row of identical stucco houses until they somehow found their own. Often, to break up the monotony, they would chart a new course through the numerical and alphabetic grid of streets, offering them slightly different sameness.

One day they saw Edward Kovacs walking home on the other side of the street. He was a quiet, bespectacled kid who kept to himself and seemed born of another era. He kept his wavy hair parted on the side and always seemed to be wearing too much clothing; all of it muted grays and browns. His family had just moved from Hungary and although he could speak English, he rarely spoke outside of the classroom.

At school Edward was made fun of a lot, but he was also a practiced chameleon able to disappear into the surroundings whenever he wanted to. Blake and his cronies would occasionally jump on the bandwagon and mock his timidity, but for the most part they wanted to try to shape him into an American boy.

"Hey Eddie," shouted Blake across the street. "Wanna walk with us? We're going to Sun Valley Dairy on the way home to get a frosty."

Eddie pushed his glasses back up to the bridge of his nose and swept his angularly cut bangs back across his forehead. He looked like a miniature version of an Eastern European scientist. "My mom says I'm not supposed to eat sweets before dinner," he said. Blake and his friends laughed, and with his husky voice Luke shouted, "Its 3:30 Kovacs, what time does your mom serve up the goulash?" They all giggled and Luke gave Blake an elbow. They laughed a little more and then waved him over.

"She doesn't like goulash," said Edward as he began to cross the street. He was looking left to right with each step, checking for traffic, a rarity in this neighborhood. He joined the three boys and gave them a smirky smile that had become his trademark. It was as though a full smile would be too indulgent.

"Jeez, do you go anywhere without that thing?" asked Blake. He was staring at the black clarinet case in Edward's hand. Edward seemed ashamed and didn't reply. He was an extremely talented clarinetist and played in both the school orchestra and jazz band, but even this brought him ridicule.

The boys climbed the hills that radiated eastward from their school until they reached the Sunset Reservoir. It was an eight-square-block county reservoir that was built into a hillside. The facility was surrounded by a mile of chain link fence and the boys often walked along its shrub-lined perimeter as a shortcut to the Sun Valley Dairy.

As they walked next to the fence they let their fingers rub against it, creating an almost musical sound.

Blake stared at the flat concrete expanse that was the roof of the reservoir. It was built with the same lack of creativity as the rest of the neighborhood. At certain points they could hear the mysterious rush of water, torrents pouring from, and into, the unknown. They would pause and listen for a second or two and then quickly move on, their minds racing with morbid conjectures.

They were nearly at the corner, their soft serve ice cream only a mere block away, when they noticed that someone had cut a hole in the fence.

"Let's go in," said Luke, the bravest and most reckless of the bunch.

"No way," said Ronald, his dark straight hair falling over his eyes. "We'll get busted for sure. It's wide open out there."

Blake looked around, searching for any other signs of life and was not surprised to find that they were alone. He did one more 360 and said, "This is our chance. We've always wanted a closer look, right?"

Edward looked frightened by the idea and was taking tiny steps backwards. Luke looked over at him and grabbed him by the arm. "This is going to be awesome, Eddie. No kid will ever make fun of you after today. Come on."

"Do you really think so?" said Edward. Luke shook his head and Edward stepped through the hole in the fence before anyone else, leaving the other boys scrambling to be next.

Once they were on the other side they stood on the asphalt service road that surrounded the immense concrete plateau. There was what appeared to be an access door leading into the reservoir a couple of hundred feet away. It rose up from the barren plain like an entrance to a bunker or bomb shelter. Blake gave the signal to run to the alcove for cover.

The four boys ran, afraid but smiling. When they reached the door they huddled in the shallow alcove and Luke unsuccessfully tried to open the padlock. Edward, still holding his clarinet case, seemed warm in his long grey coat but his smile had filled out and he was obviously lost in the moment of inclusion.

They peeked around the corner and Blake could see that there was a pathway cutting through the middle of the reservoir, cleaving it into two similar halves. The pathway seemed to dip down below the roofline and he thought it would provide good cover for their "recon mission", whatever it turned out to be.

They ran to the mouth of the pathway in groups of two, Blake and Edward reaching it first. The boys reconvened and started down the service path together, catching their breath. They were surprised to find small screened openings along either side of the two reservoir halves and guessed they were vents.

"Whoa. Can we see inside there?" asked Luke.

"I'm not sure I want to," said Ronald.

Luke started making chicken sounds and the other boys laughed, Edward included.

"Hey. We're not even supposed to be in here, dumb ass," Ronald added.

"We better keep moving," said Blake.

About two hundred feet further on, Blake saw it. One of the ventilation screens was missing. The reservoir and its untold murk were open to the world. "Hey you guys. Check it out," he said, pointing to the rectangular gap, just big enough for a body to fit through. "I have to look in."

Blake boosted himself up to the opening that sat just above their heads. He leaned in, supporting himself with his arms. "Oh wow," his voice said with a reverberating echo. "It's like a giant lake in here. A big, giant, underground lake."

"Let me see," said Luke, tugging on one of Blake's belt loops. The boys swapped places and Luke poked his head in. "Whoa. It's so big you can't even see the other side," he said. He lingered at the opening. "Hey, my eyes are adjusting to the dark. There's a ledge in here. Let's climb inside and see if we can all sit inside."

"No way," said Ronald.

Luke started making the chicken sounds again and they bounced off the water like a skipping rock. He climbed up and disappeared into the opening. Everyone fell silent. They stared at each other for a moment and then curiosity finally won over and the boys all tried to pull themselves up at the same time, even Edward, clarinet case clenched in one fist. One by one they entered the cavernous space, their every move amplified and echoed by the still water.

"Holy shit," said Ronald, the boys laughing as the words echoed across the massive basin.

"Scoot down," said Blake as he saw Edward still only halfway into the opening, struggling with his case.

The three boys got up from their perch on the narrow ledge and awkwardly crawled along, unable to stand with the enormous roof only three feet above them. They were just beginning to reseat themselves on the tiny shelf when they heard a huge splash. It was the last sound any of them wanted to hear. Blake turned toward the water. Edward had fallen in as he pulled himself into the reservoir housing, sliding right over the edge and into the water.

"Eddie," screamed Blake. The faint light from the dozens of ventilation panels revealed the boy struggling to stay afloat in the dark holding pond. A cacophony of panicked screams bounced across the water as the boys shouted instructions to Edward who was still clutching his clarinet case. He tried to make his way back to the ledge but his wet heavy clothing was pulling him downward. "I can't swim. Please. Help me."

Below the surface of the water, Edward was desperately trying to keep his feet on the steep slope that formed one of the four sides of the reservoir basin. But the sides of the deep pool were covered with years of algae, and he kept sliding back down into the cold water. He would become invisible to the other boys as he slid farther out, into the black void, into deeper water. His pleading for help yielded to choked cries and the boys heard him spit out mouthfuls of water.

Waves of fear engulfed the boys. Luke and Ronald moved closer to the hole that they climbed in through and began screaming for help. Edward's thrashing began to slow. Blake lay on his stomach on the small ledge and called to him, "Eddie, try and grab my hand." He repeated it several times as he held his arm out above the abyss. No reply came, save for his own echo. A hush fell over the boys as they collectively listened for Edward. Nothing.

Suddenly they saw something moving toward them in the water, and a glimmer of hope returned. "Eddie?" asked Ronald. The object began to materialize in the faint light and the boys let out a scream. They clawed their way toward the vent opening, a panic of kicking legs and arms as they exited the reservoir, save for Blake who was still lying there with his arm out, his cheeks wet with tears as the clarinet case drifted into view.

From the back seat of the cab Blake stared out dumbly, wishing that San Francisco's changed skyline would distract him enough to halt the flood of memories that continued to breech the dam. But the novelties could not usurp his own history and he was sucked back in time to the reservoir again, to the neighborhood he had all but erased from his mind.

He remembered how they had huddled in horror before fleeing the scene, hiding within a group of bushes just outside the reservoir fencing. Blake recalled how in their young minds they were certain they would be blamed for the accident. With trembling voices they each vowed a code of silence and then walked away without looking back. In the days after Edward's death they spoke to one another very little, other than to measure the resolve of the other two.

Blake remembered arousing suspicion with his parents when he suddenly refused to drink tap water or even shower or bathe in it. He said he was worried about it being polluted, sitting in the old concrete reservoir. His father told him that the reservoir was only for emergencies and that they monitored the water quality anyway, which was both a relief and a worry.

There was a massive search but the boys were never questioned by police, and no one ever discovered Edward Kovacs' body, so the whole event sank deeper and deeper into a protective chamber within Blake's mind until it was, at least on a conscious level, forgotten.

The taxi exited the freeway turning onto Monterey Boulevard, heading west. Blake looked ahead and caught the eyes of the driver in the rear view mirror. "Twenty-fifth and Taraval?" the driver asked, without turning his head from the road.

"Twenty-fourth," Blake replied.

The coastal fog met the car as they approached the outside lands and a familiar claustrophobia invaded Blake. Soon the car was in front of the hundred-year-old brick building. It looked like an armory, afforded with few windows and a thick massive door.

"Taraval Station," the driver announced proudly as he pulled in front.

Blake paid the man and climbed the terrazzo steps. The reservoir lay a mere three blocks to the north. Once inside he was met by a long counter under a wall of bullet proof glass. He took a deep breath and trepidly approached the glass. An officer in his fifties got up from his desk and walked up to his side of the counter, a two inch thick piece of glass between him and Blake. He turned on the intercom and flatly said, "How can I help you?"

MOUNTAINOUS

Sarah was typically a calm person but her voice was trembling, devoid of its normal lilt. "How many are out there?" she asked. Gordon paused before answering; he knew she would want an exact count. The thick rain made it difficult to see out the windows so he whispered the numbers as he pointed at each figure, like a child solving arithmetic on a blackboard.

"I would say eleven or twelve now." He could sense his wife's mounting unease and hoped that the number would have been less, but it kept increasing as the hours went by. He thought about lying, but after four decades of marriage she would have known.

Gordon turned from the window and saw that she was standing nervously in the center of the dimly lit living room, away from the windows. He could see that she clearly no longer knew what to do with herself. The sky grew darker and the weak light from the dying fire began to dance faintly upon the pine walls of the cabin. Earlier he decided it would be better to be cold than to expose themselves by throwing on another log on the fire.

"Come on, Sarah. We don't really know what they want. We can't just assume that they mean us harm," he said.

"Well, why are they just standing out there in the rain?" she asked.

Gordon had no explanation. He was equally vexed, equally afraid. It was as though the rain itself was changing the quiet community.

Decades ago, he and Sarah had purchased one of the first cabins to be built on the mountain. It was part of a development of seasonal homes that were built around a small lake. Gordon estimates that they have spent more than thirty summers at the cabin. He liked that it gave them access to an unhurried lifestyle and felt that was important for their children when they were growing up, something they couldn't get in the city. Now, no longer bound by the school calendar, they lingered in their mountain retreat well into the fall.

Gordon looked at his wife of forty one years. She seemed so small and frail standing there in the middle of the room, like a frightened animal. Even the tiny rose motif on her pin-tuck shirt appeared wilted.

Gordon dug up a memory from a summer long past in the hopes that it would help calm her. "You remember that time Johnny was afraid to go outside after he saw the stag horn beetle crawling up the window?" He let out a laugh, but he knew it sounded fake. "We just told him to wait until morning and it would be gone, back to its own cozy home."

"But these are people, not insects," she said. "And they are just standing out there, in the cold rain, unmoving. There is something wrong, don't you see?" Gordon knew she was right. The first figure appeared at the edge of the woods about fifteen minutes after it started raining, now two hours later there were a dozen. And he had no idea how many more were out back.

He was frightened, but he tried to not show it. Sarah's fear was growing by the minute. Even in the fading daylight he could see that her face held so much worry. All the lines that she collected from life, from their life together, were bunched tightly around her still delicate features. He wanted to soothe her, but settled on trying to protect her from some of the details—like how one of the figures he had seen near the house appeared to be a child, holding a rusty garden spade in its hand.

Gordon walked over to his wife, gently pulling her clenched fists away from her chest. He grasped her arms loosely and looked at her with a forced calm. "You know one of the sheriff's deputies will be here any minute, right Sarah? You made the call yourself."

"But that was over an hour ago," she said without looking up. "I could hear so many telephones ringing the background, they sounded overwhelmed." She put her hands on his chest and sighed in a way that led him to believe that she would soon cry. "Oh, what do they want?" she said, the words stumbling over her staccato breaths.

Gordon hugged her and hoped she wouldn't feel the kitchen knife he had put in his jacket pocket. "Now come on, hon. It's going to be alright," he said. "Has anybody tried to get in, or even come up to the door? No. It's going to be ok."

With his arms still around her he glanced over her shoulder. Through one of the rear windows, he could make out the black silhouette of a man standing between two pine trees not thirty yards off. The man was barely discernible from the washed out landscape, grey and almost featureless.

"Lucky thirteen," Gordon whispered, too softly for her to hear.

The rain that continued to pelt the cabin carried with it a faint odor that permeated the old timbers of their home. It was an odd smell, synthetic, Gordon thought, a little like the overheated brakes of a truck coming down a mountain.

"What did the person on the phone say again?" he asked. He had been so busy locking windows and reinforcing doors that he hadn't really been paying attention to Sarah when she got off their old rotary phone. There was no cell service on the mountain.

Sarah dried her eyes with the tips of her fingers, then sat down of the edge of the rustic coffee table a few feet away. She took a tissue from the box at the center of the table and blew her nose. "Well," she sniffled. "The woman said that they were all tied up dealing with some huge explosion over at the copper mine in Wildcat Gorge."

"Oh crap. That's what, thirty miles from here?"

"Oh, I don't think it's that far … twenty at the most. She said that rescue crews were coming from all over the tri-county area because the chemical tailing dam, whatever that is, was burning out of control." Sarah paused. "Maybe the rain has already put out the fire?"

Gordon didn't respond and he watched her fleeting optimism fade away.

"The woman did say that she would send over a deputy as soon as possible to check out our situation, but that it could take up to an hour because they have very few people available. Close all the windows and stay inside was the last thing she said." Sarah began to cry. "They're not coming are they?"

Gordon sat down beside her on the edge of the coffee table and put his arm around her. "Sure they are, babe. They always come."

The two of them sat with heavy heads staring at the braided rug under their feet. Sarah was the first to break the silence. "Maybe Sophia's been right the whole time. We should have sold this place." Gordon's hands tightened and he looked at Sarah from under his brow. Their daughter, Sofia, had been concerned about their safety for the last few years. The cabin is several miles from the nearest hospital and often no one knows that they are there.

"The day my children tell me what to do is still a long way off, Sarah. I'll sell this place when I'm damn ready. And I'll decide when I need to stop having martini's before dinner too." Gordon laughed at himself. He didn't know if they were going to make it through the night and he was getting worked up about trivial things. Guess it takes our minds off of the situation he thought.

He watched his wife stare at the floor, lost in thought. "It seems just like yesterday that John and Sophia were playing on this very rug," she said.

"Yeah, Johnny would get so angry when his little sister paraded her dolls around on top of his fire truck. This table we're sitting on was the firehouse, remember?"

"I do. I remember everything we did here, the cuts and scrapes, the laughing and playing, the fighting—now they're thousands of miles away."

"Raising their own families."

"I know. I'm so glad they're not here right now."

"Me too."

Gordon took Laura's hand and he could feel the moist tissue she held balled in her palm. He thought about all the challenges they'd been through in life and how they would make it through this too, whatever it turned out to be.

Suddenly, he could see what appeared to be headlights coming down their drive. He lumbered up from the table and walked to the window near the front door. Laura followed, and through the silver curtain of rain they could see a sheriff's cruiser slowly navigating the gravel drive. The car backed into the carport beside their sedan. Gordon could hear the muffled sound of a dog barking from within the car. It was a K-9 unit that had responded to their call.

He watched with relief as the sheriff's deputy began searching their property with the cruiser's spotlight. He and Laura gasped out loud when the powerful light cut through the grey threads of rain. Near to the house as many twenty men, women, and children stood in the pouring rain, like they were rooted in the ground. They didn't run or shield their eyes from the bright light. They just stared from under their brows, waiting.

Even through the viscous rain their nearly washed out features bore an unsettling malevolence. Sarah tightened her grip on Gordon's arm. "Oh my God, Gordy. What is happening? Who are those people? What is God's name is wrong with them?"

"Wait a minute" said Gordon. "The man near the dogwood tree, isn't that Ron Parker from Rizzo's Market?" He pointed so Sarah could see. He had know Ron for years. "I just saw him a couple of days ago, good man. I'll bet he's just lost in the rain."

With that Gordon unlocked the window and threw it open. "Ron. Hey, Ron," he yelled. Before he could say another word Sarah slammed the window back down and turned the latch.

"What are you doing?" she said. "Can't you see that he is not himself? None of them are. I don't care how well you regard him, he is not your friend now."

He could see the resolve in her eyes and behind that the truth. He nodded and they turned to look back out the window. This time they were met by the cold stares of the shadowy figures outside. Each dull human form had turned to face the window that Gordon had yelled from.

"Oh, Sarah, I'm sorry," he said. "I'm so sorry."

At that moment the deputy began to address the mob through the vehicle's p.a. system. "Attention. You are trespassing and are in violation of Penal Code 602. You must cease and desist or you will be arrested. Disperse now." He repeated his speech, but the ashen figures remained unmoving, like they were adhered to the wet ground.

Gordon could see now that at least half of the figures were holding random tools and weapons in their hands—scissors, hammers, broken tree limbs. Sarah grabbed him by the sleeve and he could feel her nails digging into his arm. He watched as the light came on in the car and the deputy opened the rear door. Out jumped a large German Shepherd, alert, at the ready. The muscular dog stood at the edge of the carport, as though it were awaiting a command. Then, suddenly, it lunged into the rain, barking savagely.

The dog ran toward the nearest man, not more than forty feet from the carport. Before it was halfway to him it slowed to a stop and stood in the rain. Gordon thought he heard it let out a whimper. The dog slowly turned to face the police car and ceased moving, save for a rippling snarl. The deputy rolled down his window and called to the dog, directing his spotlight toward the animal, but it stood anchored to the gravel drive like a statue, staring into the beam of light.

Gordon realized that one of the shadowy figures had made its way into the carport and was standing next to the deputy's car. It lunged at him through the open window and within seconds the remaining dull figures had uprooted themselves and descended upon the deputy en masse. Gordon felt Sarah's grip tighten, cringing with terror as the man's screams could be heard above the horrific thuds and clang of metal. The horn began to honk spastically as the car rocked from side to side.

"Oh, dear God. We've got to help him," Sarah said. She began to punch at Gordon's chest. "Make them stop. Oh, please make them go away."

"There is no helping him, Sarah," he said as he caught her flailing arms. "He's as good as dead."

It was as though a glacial ice spread throughout the cabin as Gordon's words hung in the air. Still holding her slender wrists, he pulled her away from the window and led her through the dark hallway to the base of the stairs. They blindly made their way up the stairway and he could hear her weeping, swallowing her sobs. "We have to try to keep it together, Sarah," he said. "We have to try."

They fumbled their way through the darkness to the small bedroom at the back of the house. It was the room that their children had shared when they were young. They kept the room unchanged, bunk beds and all, for their grandchildren to use during family visits. One small window overlooked the forest, and a dim nightlight glowed faintly in one corner.

Gordon led his wife to the lower bunk and helped her lay down upon the small bed. She curled up into a sort of fetal position, and began to gently rock herself. "Are we going to die tonight? At the hands of those demons?" she asked. "Or even worse, become like them?"

She was shaking, so he made his way to the closet and retrieved a blanket. He covered her and sat on the edge of the bed and stroked the length of her arm. In a soft voice he said, "No, love, we're not going to die tonight. Or tomorrow. When morning comes, we're going to drive out of here like Jehu."

Sarah grabbed his arm. "I'm still in love with the man I met all those years ago," she said.

Gordon, smiling, took her hand in his and knelt by the bed. "I have to go back downstairs to double check the windows and doors. Then I'm going to pack us a bag so we can leave at the drop of a hat. I think it would be foolish to try to leave before this rain lets up, before those things …" He quickly rephrased. "It will be safer to have the sun on our side so let's plan on making our break first thing in the morning. Hell, maybe they will have moved on. You get some rest, I'll be right back." He couldn't see his wife's face but he stroked her moist cheeks gently with the back of his hand. "Ok?" he said.

"Yes," she said. "I don't want to be alone but I'm no help to you right now. You go on. But come back as soon as you're finished."

Gordon leaned forward, gave her a kiss, and ambled into the darkness. Downstairs, he suddenly became engulfed with feelings of helplessness, of being powerless, and he began to cry. He had no idea what was happening, what to do. His only plan was to flee when the time came. His knew his responsibility was to protect Sarah. There was no way he could fight off the growing mob outside.

He crawled from room to room on his hands and knees to avoid detection, checking the lock on each window. He slowed when he reached the window by the front door and he peered in the direction of the deputy's vehicle. There wasn't a soul around. The engine was running and the wipers were streaking across the broken windshield. He recognized that the blood stain was on the inside, the wipers unable to move it away.

The rain looked yellow and sickly in the headlights and the strange odor wafted in through the gaps around the doorjamb. Gordon moved on, crawling toward their bedroom on the first floor. They had converted the den into a master suite years ago to avoid climbing the stairs. With the fire dead and the sun gone, the cabin was now completely black. His knees creaked in unison with the antique pine floor as he crept down the dark hallway.

Once in the bedroom he found his way to the closet. He could feel the small duffle bag in the corner and he blindly stuffed some of his clothes into the bag before turning to Sarah's side of the closet. He could smell the faint scent of soap, or perfume, he didn't know which, but he found comfort in it just the same. He carefully folded some of her garments in the dark and placed them in the bag.

Gordon then crawled on to the bathroom to gather what he thought would be necessary sundry items. He kept expecting to hear a thump at the door, or the crash of breaking glass, but there was no sound from outside, except for the rain. Even that had diminished slightly. Once he found what he wanted he ascended the staircase like a four-legged animal, duffle over his shoulder.

When Gordon entered the rear bedroom and whispered his wife's name, there was no reply. The nightlight had been turned off and he couldn't see the bed. Worry began to pump through his veins. He felt his way to the bed and could feel Sarah's motionless body on top. She had fallen asleep.

There was some protective mechanism in Sarah that just shut her body down after a crisis. She told him of how she found her mother dead in the kitchen when she was a child, and how she slept for days afterward, even missing the funeral. He had seen it before himself, like the time Sarah got into a car accident while driving their son John to school. Once she returned home, she slept all day and all night.

There was no reason to wake her now, he thought. Gordon quietly placed the duffle bag at the foot of the bed and lay down beside her on the narrow bed, still wearing his coat for warmth. In the morning he figured either they would make a run for it, or if they couldn't, another deputy would be dispatched to find their fallen brother. He checked for the knife in his pocket, and fell asleep with his face in her hair.

Gordon rose with the sun. The usual din of songbirds had been replaced with a deafening silence. He turned, looking for his wife, and saw her at the small window overlooking the back of their property. Gordon struggled to his feet, his legs stiff from the cold. Before he could tell her to move away from the window she turned and announced, "They're gone. It has stopped raining, and they're gone, Gordy." She smiled at him.

"It could be that you just can't see them. Move away from the window, will you?"

She obliged and sat next to him on the tiny bed. "I don't even know what to think," she said. "Was it real? Did it really happen?"

Gordon knew they'd have their answer as soon as they saw the deputy's car. "Listen, love. We need to get out of here now, while it's not raining and those people are not surrounding our cabin. I packed us a bag so let's get on our way. I don't plan on stopping till we're home."

Gordon stood up and picked up the bag. "The further away from here the better. You can call the sheriff's office from your cell phone once we're off the mountain. And after that maybe you should call a realtor." He paused, and they let out a little laugh, both of them drunk with the joy of living another day.

They walked down the stairs and Sarah said, "Should we call the kids too?"

"They probably already heard about it from the media. Come on, let's get out of here." At the bottom of the stairs Gordon directed Sarah to a little bench near the front door. He knew from there the deputy's cruiser would be out of her line of sight. "You wait here while I fetch the car. Don't get up until I call for you, ok?" He didn't want her to see what had transpired last night, now clearly visible in the light of day.

Gordon took a look out of the window and saw no one around. He opened the door a little, then a lot, and stepped outside. He took the kitchen knife out of his pocket and slowly walked across the wet gravel toward the carport. The ground was slick, as though it were covered in oil. He made frequent stops to see if any surprises were coming his way. The sky was partly cloudy but it looked like the storm had moved on. He heard a flutter from somewhere and brought the knife in front of him. He was relieved upon finding it to be only a dove. It was shaking its wings convulsively from under a nearby tree.

As Gordon approached the carport he began to survey the destroyed cruiser. It lay like a mortally wounded creature, its dim, fading headlights like dying eyes. The engine had run out of gas but the wipers continued to make a pathetic arc across the shattered windshield, unable to wipe away the blood on the inside. "Sorry, Sarah," Gordon said aloud. "It wasn't a bad dream." Now, standing in between the two cars, Gordon could see traces of blood and entrails leading into the woods behind the carport. Shredded clothing lay everywhere, like the deputy's uniform had been furiously ripped to pieces. Gordon picked up his pace, not wanting to spend another second next to the carnage. He shuddered and opened the door to his sedan.

He started the engine, and out of habit, let it warm for a few seconds. He slowly pulled away from the carport and noticed that the cloud cover had thickened, the sky slightly darker now. Gordon pulled up in front of the house and, leaving the engine running, ran in to get Sarah. She met him at the door with their bag in her hand and they hurried to the car. Gordon thought he felt a drop of rain hit his face. He instinctively held his hand over her head as she got in the car. He looked around the property and all was still, no one in sight.

He got in the car and glanced back at the cabin. "Oh, Christ," he said. "We forgot to shut the door." Their summer home had become such a part of them that they couldn't just drive away with the front door open to the world. "Hold on," he said as he got out of the car.

"Hurry," she said.

Gordon walked briskly to the cabin. He fumbled with the keys and was angry at himself for still being nervous. He locked the front door and turned. He looked up at the clouds and his expression was almost one of pain. The sky had become black. As soon as he stepped off the porch it started pouring. Pale yellow rivulets of rain began to stream down the windows of the car. "Gordon," he heard Sarah call from within.

He pulled his coat over his head and started running toward the car. His attempt to protect himself from the rain was failing. His pace began to slow. Midway to the car he stopped moving, his coat falling from his head and settling back onto his shoulders. He stood there not three feet from the car, staring at Sarah from under his brow. His hand was coiled into a fist inside his coat pocket.

"No… no," Sarah cried out. She reached over and locked the driver's side door. She turned to lock the rear doors and in doing so could see the bag Gordon had packed in the back seat. It was only partially zipped and she could see her hair brush lying atop her neatly folded clothes. A tear came to her eye. Even after so many years of life's ups and downs she knew they still really loved each other. She glanced at the keys in the ignition of the still idling car and then buried her face in her hands, weeping, not knowing what to do. After several minutes she lifted her head. No more tears fell. Gordon was still standing in the rain, like a stone sculpture. Without a moment's hesitation she opened the door and got out of the car. Her eyes fixed upon his and they stood, unblinking.

Together.

DRAWBRIDGE

Caz wasn't his full name but it was a lot less cumbersome than Cazenovia. The other problem he had with his name was that everyone always seemed let down when they discovered it wasn't Casanova. Their smiles would simply fade away. He hated his hippy parents for it, even now in his mid-twenties.

He played the message again. "Mr. Casanova? Oh, wait, hold on. I'm sorry. Mr. Cazenovia Pierce? My name is Rebecca Gad; I'm an editor at the *Oakland Tribune*. We're doing a five-year anniversary piece on the ghost town, Drawbridge, and we understand you were one of the last residents to leave there back in 1979. We were hoping to interview you and maybe take some photos of you in your old house. Please give me a call at …" Beep. Caz stopped the playback; he was running late for work.

On his way to McNally's Builders Supply, where he worked as a forklift driver, he picked up a package of powdered donuts and a coffee from 7-Eleven. He arrived at his job fifteen minutes late, which was the norm. He remembered being late on his first day, how another employee had called him on it. Caz laughed. Gotta train them right away, he thought.

He climbed atop the lemon-yellow forklift, his "throne", and went about his morning routine of loading and unloading units of plywood. The portable radio next to his seat was blasting Def Leppard as he moved the lift around the yard like he was part of an industrial ballet. After an hour he switched the machine off and started to eat his last donut. Reagan was on the radio talking about his disappointment in Russia's boycott of the Summer Olympics. Caz leaned back in the taped-up vinyl seat and gave a salute to his boss, who was passing by, and then rolled his eyes when Gerry doubled back to talk to him.

"Hey, Caz. You're good with your hands," he said. It was the classic prelude to someone asking a favor. Gerry adjusted the glasses he was wearing, which were too big for his face. "Can you take a look at the coffee machine in the break room today?" It was one of those coin-operated vending machines, and the flow of coffee had slowed to a trickle. He was happy to look at it since he was the number one coffee drinker and his hand was starting to hurt from punching the constipated leviathan every day. "Ask Hayden to help you," Gerry added.

Caz didn't like Hayden. Nobody liked Hayden. Gerry had hired him from some halfway house he'd learned about through his twelve-step program and had given him the coveted job of yard manager, angering all the long-time employees. Hayden was older than the rest of the crew and asserted his newfound authority at every opportunity. He had wide-set, unblinking eyes and he carried on at length about his time on a submarine during the "war". They were always the same old stories—near death experiences, "rats as big as Dobermans," shirtless men covered in grease.

Once Caz had taken a peek at a photocopy of Hayden's driver's license in the office and had seen that his age didn't really line up with any war. Caz didn't trust him and avoided him at all costs, going the other way whenever he saw him coming. He knew that his boss, Gerry, was having substance and marital problems, but his perpetual gullibility was perhaps his real weakness.

In the break room Caz had the front of the vending machine off and was tracing the hose from the coffee making apparatus to the spigot that dispensed the brew into cups. "I think if we remove this hose, we'll find the problem," he said to Hayden, who was comparing the machine to something on a Navy sub. He was one of those people who stopped working as soon as he started talking, like every word needed the fullest attention. Caz nodded robotically, waiting for a break in the rant. None came so he finally had to interrupt, "Can you just hand me the flat-head screwdriver?"

Caz unscrewed the hose clamp and pulled off the tube. What looked like coffee beans seemed to have become lodged in the yellowed hose. He put it up to his lips and gave it a big blow. From the other end dozens of cockroaches came shooting out. Most were dead, but not all.

Hayden ran out of the room and Caz started yelling "abandon ship, abandon ship." He was laughing hysterically, but as he watched the roaches scurry across the linoleum floor, soggily searching for cover, he could feel his breakfast coming up. Suddenly, Hayden's flight didn't seem as funny and he started spitting onto the floor, trying to purge the perceived taste of roach. "Damn it," he said. "I drink twenty to thirty cups of that crap a week."

Caz had knocked off work early, citing nausea, and stopped at the Liquor Locker on his way home. Old Crow tasted more like medicine than bourbon, he thought. Surely it could disinfect the roach shit he'd been ingesting on a daily basis. He took a swig from the pint, still sheathed in its brown paper bag, and set his keys down on the cherry wood table that he inherited from his grandfather. He suddenly remembered the unusual message that the reporter had left for him and stared unblinkingly at the answering machine. How the hell had they found him? Weird.

In the three weeks since his roommate Daniel moved out, no one had called—except for Daniel. "Did I leave my flush-trim router bit there? I can't find my coping saw. Did you borrow it?" Daniel apprenticed at a woodworker's collective in Berkeley. Initially he and Caz bonded over their shared interest in woodworking. They became caught up in a sort of whirlwind romance, sharing tools and stories, collaborating on weekend projects. At night they sat at the kitchen table flipping through woodworking magazines, sighing wanton sighs, like it was porn.

Then one day, the flame went out. At least for Caz. After he built a drum platform for his drum set he pushed his tools aside and set up his kit in the garage. This was his real true love, and Daniel felt betrayed. By the time Caz's metal band, Sintax, started rehearsing in the former shrine that was their garage, the man-crush was over. Caz came home one day to a note on the table and an empty bedroom down the hall.

He took another gulp of bourbon and thought about writing a new ad for a roommate. Then he thought about how much he liked the sound of the woman's voice on his answering machine. Her throaty voice was worthy of a replay. And her last name, Gad, sounded like some foreign word for a sexual act, so he pressed play and let his mind paint her a face.

"Why do you care about that shithole?" he whispered as her message played back. His memories of Drawbridge and the family cabin were mostly unpleasant. Still, he wasn't going to shy away from potential fame, no matter how insignificant it was. After the message ended he took one more swallow of whiskey, this time for courage, and dialed the number she had left for him. If anything, he might be able to get her to include something about the band in the article.

Caz had phoned in sick earlier in the morning. As far as he was concerned, McNally's owed him the day off after poisoning him for months with roach-infused coffee. He had just received the official call from Rebecca saying that the meeting was on. "Ok. I can meet you there in about an hour and a half, at noon," he said. "Will that work?" She, an intern, and the staff photographer had arranged to meet him by the railroad tracks that bisected Drawbridge. "Sounds good," he said, still not believing that he would be returning to the mire. "Goodbye."

On his drive to Fremont, Caz was already digging into the pack he had prepared for his hike to Drawbridge. It was a six mile trek from the point he would set out from, all of it on awkwardly spaced railroad tracks. "Man's gotta have fuel," he said. He turned up the radio when a Judas Priest song came on and he sang along with a mouth full of salami.

He exited the highway and drove west down the old familiar parkway until the road just kind of slowly disappeared, becoming one with the red dust that emanated from the quarry at the end of the road. The dust settled over everything within fifty feet, creating the perfect portal into no man's land. He pulled over, grabbed his pack and hopped out. He locked up his Dodge Colt and set off down the railroad tracks as he had hundreds of times before, into the vaporous marshlands.

Caz had hated every life-abating moment he'd spent on Drawbridge. From the weekends he spent there when he was young, as the unwanted appendage on his parents' "free" lifestyle, to the soul-crushing year he lived there as an adult. When he was a boy his parents often used the cabin as a retreat for weekend "happenings." He had no idea at the time what this meant but as he got older he pieced together that they and their friends spent the weekend getting high and jumping into bed with each other. This created a preponderance of alone time for Caz as a boy, and he kept busy fishing and exploring the surreal island outpost in the middle of nowhere.

He picked up his pace, walking briskly down the tracks while he worked out new drum riffs in his head.

Every step he took set off an explosion of tiny flies trying to flee his approaching shadow. Caz could feel them getting stuck up his pant legs. "God, I hate it here," he mumbled. He reached inside his pack and fumbled around for his Walkman and the demo tape that he and Sintax recorded a few months earlier. With newfound enthusiasm, he placed them back in his pack and hopped up onto a rail, walking it like a balance beam.

He knew Rebecca and her crew had an even longer walk, coming from Alviso to the south. But it was a safer route to the marshy island that Drawbridge was slowly sinking into, with a foot path running parallel to the train tracks. That is why he had recommended it to her. Besides, he wanted to get to the deserted settlement first, to survey the damage that was his former home, California's youngest ghost town.

In the distance, about a quarter mile ahead, he could see a faint boxy shape with a light on it. It looked like a small building, but he knew it was Amtrak's Capital Corridor on its way to Sacramento. Even after a year of living less than fifty feet away from the tracks he still couldn't believe how quiet the massive northbound diesels were when standing directly in their path. Without the blast of a horn, only the faint creaking of timber could be heard under the rails. Most of the engines heading north pushed the train cars rather than pulling them, making them almost silent until they were directly upon anyone who might be walking the tracks. This included Amtrak's formidable Coast Starlight, which was no louder than an oscillating table fan.

Silent death, he thought, as he continued to walk toward the approaching passenger train. Despite the repeated blare of the air-horn, he waited until the last second before jumping off the tracks and onto the gravel slope that surrounded the berm. He thought that he recognized the engineer but the man just scowled at Caz, making him feel embarrassed by the prank. These guys had always been nice to him, and some would even stop to give him a lift if he waved a white flag from his cabin. Caz guessed they had probably just felt sorry for him.

He came to the bridge over the Mud Creek Slough. Halfway across he opted to walk a straight line down the middle of the bridge to avoid stepping on the newly beheaded raccoon lying on each side of the tracks. There was no way out if you found yourself on the bridge when a train was coming, even for a coon. You could jump into the slough, but the broken stilts of former fishing shacks made it look like an impaling garden.

Once over the bridge, Caz could see the remains of the family cabin in the distance. It had been built in the early 1920s by his grandfather, Ellis, and was originally intended to be a weekend retreat for duck hunting parties. It was a tiny shack that afforded its occupants little more than a tin roof and two bunk rooms on either side of a small kitchen. As Caz walked through the reedy marsh toward the shack, he could see that most of the exterior siding had been stripped away. Miraculously, it seemed like a lot of the interior walls had remained intact. Vandals don't like Grandpa's olive green wallpaper either, he thought.

Ellis Bertrand Pierce lived for the hunt. He was one of the many lawless armed men who helped shape Drawbridge's dark past. He played a major role in the introduction of "friendly ladies" to the community, and also made sure that the settlement was "wet as a monsoon" during prohibition, thanks to the large still he built at the end of a jetty. It blew up one night and took Ellis with it. Everybody suspected foul play but there was no real authority to report the alleged crime to.

As a boy Caz would occasionally poke around in the mud with a stick, looking for the old still. Every time he hit something hard he would back off and investigate no further, his mind convinced that it was his grandfather's skull.

Walking toward the family cabin, Caz was surprised by how many of the dilapidated, looted structures were already sinking into the bay. The Sprung Hotel was reduced to a mass of slanted framing timbers, surrendering their burden to gravity and the elements. Nature doesn't waste any time, he thought. The rotting silvered wood and the rusty iron hardware mirrored the hazy sky and tawny grasses, as though an amalgamation were underway.

He reached his former home and stood motionless in the slanted doorway of the floorless and glassless structure, unable to enter. A buried bitterness began to surface and he once again thought about his parents' warped take on parenting. As freewheeling as they had been with their own lives, they had imposed their beliefs on Caz with a mutated tyranny.

His parents had sent Caz off to an artsy West Coast boarding school as soon as they could—to hide him away, he assumed. During his senior year, he received a letter from them stating that they were getting rid of all their possessions and moving to India to pursue their "spiritual rite of passage." Taped to the back of the note was a key to the cabin.

After graduating, Caz had nowhere to go and no savings to speak of, except for a few hundred dollars his grandmother squirreled away for him. So he moved into the forsaken cabin. Caz spent a tortuous, isolated year there, unable to find work until the seven month anniversary of his arrival, what he hoped would be the lowest point of his life. "It's only up from here," he would say to himself every day upon waking. He knew if he had been able to follow the path of his classmates he would already be attending college.

Other than the occasional "pity train" that would stop for Caz, he was faced with an absolute lack of transportation. His job search was confined to the two small towns that sat at either end of the railway line, his umbilical cord to civilization. He was able to hold down an afternoon paper route for a few months, but without a car the winter rains ultimately made his arduous trek impossible.

Finally, after Alviso was granted its first bus stop, he was able to broaden his search and, eventually, he landed the job at McNally's in San Jose. He awoke every day at four in the morning to walk the dark tracks, still half asleep, in order to reach the first of the two buses he needed to take. After a few months he was able to save up enough money and set out to find an apartment closer to work. He rented the first one he saw.

Caz had been the last inhabitant to leave Drawbridge. And now, standing amongst the ruins of the family cabin, he couldn't believe that he had ever lived here. "What a piece of shit," he shouted to no one, frightening a nearby blue heron, that had been honing in on a fish. The floorboards of the cabin were gone and it had sunk into the mud considerably, making the petite rooms look even smaller. Picture hooks, still fastened to the walls reminded him of all the bad hippy art that had taken the place of Grandpa's hunting photos during his parents' tenure. One sun-faded wall even bore the outline of Ellis' old gun rack. He remembered looters running off with it as he came home from his paper route one evening. If they had looked in the cabin's only closet they would have found the Remington shotgun it was made for as well.

Outside, Caz could hear the sound of an approaching train slowing to a stop. Judging by the time of day, he though it to be the Altamont Commuter. But why was it stopping here? Trains hadn't made a regular stop in Drawbridge since the 1950s. He stepped out from the doorway, from the remains of his past, into the perineal haze that surrounded the wetlands.

The idle diesel locomotive started up again and rolled from its impromptu stop, revealing two women and a man standing at the track's edge. He assumed it was Rebecca and her crew and waved in their direction, like people do when they are stranded in a place they don't want to be. "Ahoy," he said, and then wished he hadn't. They waved back and started off in his direction. Caz ambled across the muck, deftly traversing the narrow but deep rivulets that were partially obscured by pickle weed and marsh grass.

"You must be Rebecca," he said upon reaching the party. He figured it was her because she looked a little older than the other woman and more closely resembled the face he had assigned to the voice on his answering machine. Her pixie-like features and tousled punky hair lent her an almost mischievous look, which he found to be quite attractive.

"Good guess, Casanova. Oh, sorry. How do you pronounce your name?" she asked. She was blushing slightly from her faux pas and he found it to be refreshingly sincere.

"Caz will do," he said.

"Great. Caz, this is Robert. He's our staff photographer," she said pointing to the mustached man wearing an ill-fitting khaki vest. "And this is Courtney, my editorial intern," she said, putting her arm onto the shoulder of a nervous looking girl, in a white sweater and turquoise Polo shirt.

"Pleased to meet you," he said to them both.

Rebecca breathed deeply and said, "So, this is Drawbridge?"

They all surveyed the flat boggy landscape. "Yup, what's left of it," said Caz. "Belongs to the US National Wildlife Refuge now." He turned back to the group. "How do you want to do this?"

"Well, I was thinking you could give us a tour of some of the remaining structures and then we can talk while we walk," answered Rebecca.

In his head Caz heard Steven Tyler singing "Walk this way, talk this way" but chose not to share. "Sounds like a plan," he said instead.

Drawbridge had been settled in a way that made it easy to navigate in a linear fashion, all the structures having been erected less than fifty feet from the rail line. As they were walking along the tracks, with Caz playing docent, he noticed that Rebecca walked with a pronounced limp. He wasn't sure why but he found it to be equally sad and attractive. His mind quickly went over many possibilities as to its origin, but her denim skirt and boots shrouded any visual clues.

Robert meanwhile, with his Banana Republic safari outfit, broke off to begin taking photos of the detritus of a past civilization. His movements were overly dramatic, as though he felt if he didn't capture the image of a cabin quickly the shot would be gone forever. Caz held back his laughter, and for the next thirty minutes he answered Rebecca's questions about the history of Drawbridge, about the lawlessness, debauchery, and isolation.

"So, after high school you moved out here full time? What was it like?" she asked.

"It sucked," said Caz. "More than anyone could imagine. I guess that's stating the obvious though." He held his arms out offering her the view, his face mockingly bemused. "I mean, imagine what it was like just trying to get groceries. It's a six mile walk from the north, eight miles from the south. There were only two other people living out here when I moved into my grandfather's cabin. They were both in their sixties, long-time Drawbridgers who retired from society decades ago, bad teeth and bad company. Ultimately they could no longer handle the vandalism and looting. They wound up moving out a few months after I arrived." Caz laughed. "I didn't take it personal though."

"How did you survive out here? It all seems so elemental, primal."

"Fishing and duck hunting mostly, just like everyone had when they first settled this non-town. I had one of Grandpa's shotguns and borrowed a rod and reel from one of the old farts before he cleared out. I also taught myself how to make simple furniture and tools and stuff from the wood I salvaged from abandoned structures."

Caz stopped to point out one of the old duck clubs and the intern, with her head in her notebook, bumped into him. "Sorry," Courtney said without looking up. Caz pretended not to notice.

"What about water?" asked Rebecca.

"Believe it or not, they did install water pipes when they laid down the rail. The pipes were seventy years old though, with no water pressure to speak of and water that was more brown than clear. I always hoped it was just rust." His mind flashed to the coffee machine at McNally's and he shuttered. "Hey, you like music?" he asked, changing the subject.

Rebecca smirked. "Doesn't everyone?" she said, apparently surprised by the non sequitur. "Why?"

"Well I'm in a band, a heavy metal band, and I brought our demo. I thought maybe you could give it a listen." Caz was nervous. "If you like it, I mean us, Sintax, maybe you could mention the band in your article."

She pushed her hair back, letting her hand come to rest on the back of her neck. Looking at her feet she said, "Um, yeah. I can check it out. Mind if we finish talking about Drawbridge first?"

"Oh yeah, sure," he said, smiling.

They continued on, walking along the tracks, periodically exiting the iron highway to examine assorted architectural ruins. On their way back to the main path, after surveying what was left of the other hotel, which had burned down, Rebecca suddenly fell to the ground, crying out in pain. Caz and the intern ran to her side and brought the wincing reporter to her feet. "Are you ok, Becca?" asked Courtney in a worried voice.

"Yeah, I'm ok," she said, brushing the marsh grass from her skirt. She hiked it up over her knees and started massaging above her left kneecap. Caz wasn't sure if he should be looking but curiosity won out and his eyes made their way from the sky to her legs. He fought back a frown when he saw half a dozen or so pea-sized scars surrounding her knee. Were they wounds from a shotgun? He felt something stir inside him again, like he had when he first noticed her limp, equal parts sympathy and arousal.

Rebecca looked over, and seeing his expression said, "Old war wound from my partying days." She let out a self-deprecating laugh and started down the path again, her limp now more exaggerated.

"You up for some more questions, Mr. Pierce?"

"You know it," he said.

"So, the looting. What was behind that? How did anyone even know this place was here?"

He started laughing. "A local paper, not yours, erroneously pronounced the town dead in 1976." He shook his head. "Man, did they screw up. They wrote that the last residents had given up and hastily abandoned their homes, leaving valuable belongings behind. Can you believe it? What a bunch of dumb-asses. That article was the final nail in this town's coffin."

He had stopped walking, and put his hands on his hips as if to add emphasis his statement. The intern bumped into him again. "Sorry," she whispered. He again pretended not to notice and continued on. "Almost immediately it put Drawbridge on the map. Looters and vandals who made the trip weren't leaving empty handed, so they took almost everything. And when there was nothing really left to take, they started to burn things down. They were probably angry after walking all the way out here to find that they had missed out on the spoils."

Caz pointed out some of the charred remains of the shanty town, collapsed in blackened heaps like spent bonfires, slowly sinking into the bay. "By the time I showed up two years later, most of the looting had subsided. The looters had been replaced by the vandals, the curious, out to find the mystery spot. I thought about putting up flyers offering my services as a Sherpa, tack them up on some of the telephone poles in front of the Alviso station. But that's also where my nearest public phone was, seven miles away." Caz began to run down the tracks, mocking his idea, holding a finger in the air and saying, "Hold on, I'm comin'." The girls laughed, even the timid intern. He was suddenly happy he agreed to meet Rebecca in this place he had sworn he would never to return to.

"I have a question for you now, Rebecca," he said as he walked back to them. "I still don't know how you found me."

She looked a little uncomfortable and didn't answer right away. She stared at him with unsure eyes, like she was afraid she would be reopening a wound.

"From your parent's obituary," she said at last.

The mention of their death was not a surprise to Caz. He had received a letter from the Indian government a few months ago, stating that his parents were killed in a car accident. He figured that the county had received a similar notice. Still, he wished that his parents had nothing to do with the day's events, influencing his life from beyond the grave.

Rebecca's face bore genuine concern. "You knew about their deaths, right?

"Oh. Yeah. I knew."

Caz turned to face the still gray water. A flock of ducks was flying overhead and he half-expected to hear competing shotguns, as he would have when he was a boy. Today the only sound was the raspy squawking of the migrating fowl. He watched the V disappear into the horizon and then he turned back to the two women.

He felt betrayed by the moisture that was forming in his eyes. He smiled at Rebecca and then cast his gaze down the long tracks. Several yards ahead he could see Robert lying next to the rails, trying to create a dramatic wide-angle shot that would include most of the town's ghostly structures. Caz instinctively looked to the south, then back at Robert. "Uh, Bob?" he shouted. "Train." He pointed to the fast approaching monolith a quarter mile away. The photographer rolled from the tracks commando-style, even though the train wouldn't be upon him for several seconds, and began frantically taking pictures from his supine position.

"Is this guy for real?" asked Caz.

"Afraid so," she replied.

After the train passed Robert stood up, wide eyed and flush. He dusted himself off and hollered, "I think that should be the leading photo for the feature."

Caz and the two women laughed. Again he felt like he was part of something, like his former home had finally given him something to offer.

They resumed walking down the iron line toward the bridge that spanned the Coyote Creek Slough, at the southern end of the island. Caz continued to answer Rebecca's questions, but he kept his answers short, waiting for the right moment to ask her to listen to his demo tape.

He was humming one of his own tunes when they came upon what remained of the White Pelican Gun Club, which looked to be the least vandalized structure remaining. As they headed down the path toward the hovel Caz found the pause. "Hey, do you mind listening to my band's demo now?"

"Oh, right. Sure. I don't know much about heavy metal though. What's the name of your band, again?"

"Sintax."

Rebecca and Courtney smiled at each other while Caz rummaged through his pack. He withdrew a beat-up Sony Walkman, put on the headphones, and began rewinding the cassette tape housed inside. Rebecca took a seat on what remained of The White Pelican's porch, while Courtney drifted off to survey the defiant structure, its white paint still visible under the eaves.

After several fast-forward and rewind combinations, the tape was where he wanted it to be, and he handed the tattered foam headset to Rebecca. She was about to put them on when Robert came jogging up to them out of breath. "Hey, I'm still a little freaked out by the close call with the train," he said. "If it's all the same to you, I'd like to start back now."

Rebecca looked at her watch and then at Robert. His face was covered in sweat and he looked even more pale than usual. Courtney came from around the corner and fell in at Rebecca's side.

"Robert forgot his smokes in the van and he's jonesing for one now," she said to Courtney. "We'll have to go or there will be hell to pay." Robert smiled and looked down and Rebecca glanced at her watch again. "It would be good for you start entering your notes into my computer anyway."

"You have a computer?" asked Caz.

"Yes. Pretty much the entire office does now." She stood up and handed him the Walkman. It felt cold in his hand now. "I'm afraid I'll have to listen to your demo another time," she said. "I'm sorry."

Caz knew that there wouldn't be another time, so he took out the cassette and extended it to her between two fingers. "Maybe you can listen to it later?"

"That's a great idea. You don't mind leaving it with me?"

"I want you to have it. If you like it, great. Maybe you can mention us in the article, or pass it on to the right person, or … I don't know."

She took the cassette, and put it into the front pocket of her denim skirt, and the four of them started walking toward the bridge. "Caz, I can't thank you enough for your time. Drawbridge is a fascinating place, its dark past, your time here—it's so otherworldly. I'm very excited about this feature. It should run in about two weeks. We'll call you when we know the exact date."

He was still wishing she got to listen to the tape in front of him, so he could see her reaction. "Ok. Sounds good," he said.

When they reached the bridge Caz said goodbye to each of them and then turned to start his solitary journey north. After only a few dozen steps he heard a cry from behind. He turned and in the distance he could see that Rebecca had fallen while crossing the old bridge. Robert and Courtney were already helping her up, and he saw something fall from her pocket. Then he heard it, the unmistakable slap of flimsy plastic hitting the steel bridge. It was the subsequent splash that broke his heart.

"Are you ok?" he said.

"Sorry, Caz," she replied.

He walked down the tracks through the forgotten town. The flat landscape revealed no beauty, no discernable horizon. Caz stared at the steel rails beneath his feet. They were like the arteries that had fed the outpost, shuttling life to and from the unfavorable community. The web and the foot of the rails were scaly with rust but the heads were honed to a mirror-like polish, still alive. He looked down at his reflection, the empty gray behind. He never felt more at home.

THE QUICKENING
OF ETHAN BOYD

Ethan sat up and looked around. He had no recollection of the grasslands and scattered pine trees that surrounded him. A worried looking man was standing over him. Ethan vaguely recognized him as someone from his office.

"What happened?" he asked.

"You just blacked out, man. We were hiking along the trail and you just collapsed. Fell right back onto your pack, mid-sentence," said Joel.

"How long was I out?"

"Not long. Maybe five minutes? Dan ran up ahead for help. He saw a truck on one of the service roads and took off after it on foot. Brandon started off in the other direction, back the way we came, looking for any of the other teams."

Sitting on the dirt trail, Ethan rubbed his forehead and surveyed the tree-lined hills encircling the meadow. He was attempting to make sense of what had happened, but for the moment he wasn't even sure where he was. He was completely bewildered. He struggled to get to his feet. As soon as he began to lift himself off the ground he winced in pain and fell back down.

"Something's not right," he said. "My head feels like it's in a vice and …. it's like every vein in my body is constricted. I feel like my blood can't get to where it needs to be."

Joel began to fidget nervously, he was terrible in a crisis and prone to panic. "You're looking really pale. Maybe you should just wait here until Dan comes back." Ethan watched Joel's eyes move to his forearms and he followed suit. The veins in his muscular arms had taken on an abnormal reddish tint.

Ethan looked up at Joel who was now nervously searching the horizon. His sweat-stained t-shirt read, "Teamwork Trails - 2013." Ethan gradually began to recall the events of the day. He remembered that his company had organized a team-building offsite near Pescadero Creek in the foothills above Palo Alto, and he was the leader of one of the four man teams. They were on their way back to "base camp" after being the first to complete the course. He had no recollection of blacking out however, only the hole it created in his timeline.

"Do you think you should lie down, Ethan?" asked Joel. "You don't look so good."

"Bullshit," said Ethan. He rolled onto his stomach and began to push himself up. He spread his legs wide and used his knees as a fulcrum, shifting his weight back over them. He hovered there on all fours for a minute, staring down, weakened. He coughed involuntarily and a spray of blood speckled the crushed pine needles on the dirt trail below. He watched a dozen or so ants rush over to inspect the new food, only to scurry away and disappear back into the microcosm.

"Here comes a truck," shouted Joel with a sigh of relief. Ethan did his best to lift his head and watch the truck emerge from the tall trees and onto the grass-lined trail. He could see Dan's head peering out of the passenger window.

He pushed himself to a standing position and swayed like he was being held aloft by the dry summer breeze, sweet with the scent of conifer and wildflower. He felt his knees buckling under his six foot frame and fought to remain on his feet. When the ranger's truck pulled alongside, all Ethan said was, "Take me home."

Ethan's head sank into the pillow as he listened to his wife, Audrey. "I've been on the phone with Dr. Adams' office and they don't have any openings until tomorrow. They said if you feel any worse you should check yourself into the hospital."

Ethan was flat on his back, lying atop sweaty sheets. It was the day after he blacked out and he still didn't feel well. Part of him knew she was right—his wife was often his reality check. "I have meetings I can't miss today," he said. His voice was dry and weak, as if he had spent the night in a field of cottony thistle, under an arid summer sky.

"Are you kidding? Have you seen yourself?"

He knew he looked like crap, but they didn't find anything wrong with him when Dan took him to the ER on the way home. Their best guess was exhaustion, or a heat-related issue. Either way, they took blood to check for any possible infection, and said that the lab would send the results to Dr. Adams.

"Seeing him tomorrow will be fine, babe. The ER doc said I probably just need a lot of rest, which I got last night."

"It was more like a coma than sleep last night, Ethan. You didn't even move for twelve hours. And it was really weird, your skin felt so cold even though you were sweating most of the night. Feel the sheets under you," she said as she fixed her chestnut hair into a ponytail.

Ethan indulged her and slowly moved his stiff hand across the wet sheets. "I'm fine," he said. "I think I hurt my back yesterday when I fell though. Can you help me up?" This wasn't really true. He didn't know what was wrong with him but every joint was freezing up. He could see that Audrey was surprised by his asking for help. Back injury or not, Ethan never asked for help. He knew she had always regarded him as invulnerable. Most people did. He felt an indescribable stiffness as she helped pull him to his feet. It was as though his limbs were like boards held together by rusty hinges. He masked his discomfort. "You better go," he said. "You'll be late."

"Alright," she said. "The kids want to say goodbye before I drop them off at school. Connor is really worried about his daddy. He tried waking you up for breakfast earlier but you just laid there." Audrey gave Ethan a nervous smile. "He said you smelled like 'Grandma's basement'."

Ethan tried to laugh but it turned into a cough. He could taste a familiar salt on his tongue and hoped that the blood he coughed up didn't find its way out of his mouth. He was thankful Audrey hadn't noticed as she left the room to grab the kids.

Ethan, finding it hard to stand, sat on the edge of the bed. He began to gather the strength he needed to hide his illness from his two children. He still felt a bizarre constriction throughout his body, like every vein had become smaller, every muscle tighter. When he pulled up the sleeves of his pajamas, he thought the veins of his forearms looked more red than blue. His vision was a little cloudy so he wasn't sure that what he saw was entirely accurate.

Ethan could hear the excited patter of children's feet coming up the stairs and Connor and Zoë burst into the still-shuttered room. They pounced on him and he fell back onto the bed. They embraced their father and Ethan hugged them back as best he could, unable to fully bend his arms around them.

"Why do you feel so cold, Daddy?" asked his eldest, six year old Zoë.

He attempted to twirl a finger in her curly hair, trying to trace one of the loose coils. He didn't really have an answer to her question so he asked, "Does Daddy feel cold? How about Connor?" He turned to his towheaded three year old who started giggling. "Maybe we're a polar bear family?"

"I don't know," said Zoë. "Maybe?"

Ethan let out his best roar and the children laughed.

"Alright you two, downstairs you go," said Audrey, entering the room. "I told you daddy is not feeling well, so don't get too close."

Ethan released his grip and pushed himself up onto his elbows. "I love you both very much," he said. Ethan thought everything about them was so fresh and vibrant, the complete opposite of his current state.

"I love you, Daddy," said Connor.

"Me too. Feel better, Daddy," added Zoë.

He watched them run out of the room and then moved his gaze up to Audrey. She looked so concerned. "Promise me you will stay in bed today," she said.

"I can't. But I promise you I will only go into the office for my meetings, then straight home and back in bed."

Audrey touched his forehead. "I checked your temperature last night and it was normal, even a little lower than normal. Will you check it again and phone the doctor if you have a fever? They said you could talk to the advice nurse any time."

She gave him a kiss on his rough, dry lips, pulling back with a furrowed brow. "Well, I should go," she said. "The kids are going to Mrs. Wilkins' after school. I will pick them up on my way home from work, so don't do anything. Also, please don't try and drive yourself to work. Have them send a car."

"Yes, ma'am," he said, feigning a salute.

Audrey turned to look over her shoulder, smiling as she walked down the hallway. Ethan heard the front door close. He was alone in the house now. He pushed himself off the bed and let out a moan. His rigid body found its way into the bathroom. He was shocked by the man he saw in the mirror. His sallow, bloodshot eyes, set deep within his ashen face. The skin on his throat appeared to be striated like the rough bark of an evergreen tree.

He opened the medicine cabinet, took out the thermometer and put it into his mouth. He held it there just staring at the stranger in the mirror, his brown hair dry and brittle looking. Even his muscled, proud jaw betrayed him, seeming hauntingly gaunt.

The thermometer beeped and he strained to read it. It was a full two degrees below normal. He put it down on the sink, believing it to be broken. No one could sustain that temperature he thought. Ethan knew he would start to feel better soon, he just needed to make it through the day.

The company van had just dropped Ethan off at the office and he found the bright daylight to be almost unbearable. He made his way into the building and found solace within the subdued corporate color palette and tinted glass. He eventually found his desk but it was as though he was navigating through a sickly yellow fog that only he could see.

As soon as he sat down he heard a rap on his open door. It was Dan, who he considered to be a friend. Ethan was happy to see him and was thankful for his help yesterday.

"You sure had us scared yesterday," he said, pushing up his glasses. "Any idea what happened yet? Did you hear back from the doctor?"

"No, to both questions, Dan. I think I may just be exhausted." Ethan felt like he was speaking very slowly, as though the words couldn't find a clear way out. You know, job, kids, friends like you…. takes a lot of energy."

Dan laughed. "Well, thanks for leading us to victory yesterday at the off-site."

Ethan could read the worry in his friend's blue eyes. "Sure. My pleasure. I would bow but I might faint again."

Ethan hoped he was smiling but wasn't sure. His muscles were abnormally tight and as far as he could tell his facial expressions and movements seemed to come across as jerky.

"What time is our first meeting?" he asked.

Dan paused to look at his friend. "Shouldn't you be in bed? You look like shit," he said.

"Later, and thanks." Ethan concentrated and momentarily willed himself into a coherent state. "I have a duty to you and the rest of the department, so let's show them what we've got and then we can all get out of here."

"Cool. First meeting is in ten minutes," said Dan. "Want to head over to the conference room now and go over our speaking points?"

"I'll meet you there in a minute. I want to pull some materials together first."

Dan headed off to the conference room. Ethan got up and walked slowly over to his file cabinet. He had printed out some data he wanted to present at the meeting. He bent over the open drawer, searching for the file, feeling decidedly light-headed. Just make it through this, then home to bed, he thought. He found the file, closed the cabinet door, and as if for the first time, noticed the large potted plant in the corner of his office. He walked over to it and something compelled him to push his fingers deep into the wet soil. He held them there for a few seconds then pulled them out and smelled them. He closed his eyes and then put his fingers in his mouth to taste the damp soil.

Just then Dan appeared at the door. "Uh, you ok?" he asked.

"Oh. Yeah. Was just checking to see if it needed any water." He brushed his hand off against his pants and headed out the door.

The meeting wore on and Ethan let Dan do most of the talking. Ethan was starting to fade into that other place again, behind the unseen wall where everything slowed. It was like every word had to travel through several feet of earth before it reached his consciousness. He was happy that the pain had partially receded to some other place as well, subdued by a lead-like inertia.

Ethan was aware that his fatigue was becoming evident to everyone at the table. His mind was becoming so cloudy that he resigned himself to staring straight ahead, as though he were asleep with his eyes open. He could see his reflection in the wall of mirror across from him. The recessed lighting made his pale face look ghoulish. All of the sudden he started to track something on the table with his eyes. It was a large daddy-long-legs spider making it's way slowly across the conference table. Ethan held out his rigid arm, letting the spider crawl into his cupped hand. He was careful to not harm it. And then, without warning, to a chorus of gasps, he put the spider in his mouth and started chewing.

He looked at the mirror in front of him again and could see the horror on Dan's face. He watched him stand up and address the shocked faces seated at the table.

"Umm, Ethan is not feeling well today everyone. I think I better take him home. Let's try and pick up where we left off on Monday. Ethan, you should be feeling better by then, right?"

Ethan slowly nodded yes, his eyes transfixed in front of him. "I knew what I was doing but I couldn't stop," he said. "Why? Why couldn't I stop it? What's happening to me, Dan?"

A disquieting silence pervaded the room. Ethan looked around. No one would meet his eyes. They just sat quietly, looking at their laptops or the papers in front of them.

"Come on, let's go," said Dan, taking Ethan by the arm.

Ethan was back in his bed at home. He felt a little stronger and more with it, but his cognition had begun to vacillate with alarming frequency. He didn't know how long this moment of clarity would last. He looked over at Dan standing by the window, one hand to his ear, the other holding a phone.

Ethan called out to him. "Hey, Dan? Who are you talking to? I just need some sleep, man. Hang up the phone, I'm alright."

"It's Audrey," said Dan, cupping his hand over the mouthpiece. He handed the phone to Ethan.

"Hi, baby," said Ethan. He nodded his head. "No really, I'm feeling a little better." He paused as Audrey spoke. "Alright, I will call as soon as we hang up, I promise. I just need to get some sleep, and the longer I'm on the phone the less I will get." Ethan let out a laugh that turned into a cough. He looked down at the phone and wiped off the blood with a blanket. Dan had lifted a shutter and was looking out the window and Ethan was relieved that he hadn't seen what had happened. He put the phone back to his ear. "Ok, I love you too," he said. He hung up the phone, handing it back to Dan.

"Dan, thanks for driving me home. I know that was an important meeting and I can't imagine what everyone thought about what I did in there." Ethan paused, searching. "I don't even know what to think about it. I mean, it's weird. It's as though my mind and body are being hijacked and yet, for some reason, I'm kind of welcoming it. Like it's part of a bigger plan. Does that make any sense?"

"Hey, man. All I know is that you have been an outstanding leader at work and a good friend outside of work, so I'm trusting your judgment on this. If you don't think that you need to go to the hospital then I'm going to back you up. But you really do need to get some rest, you look terrible. Audrey wants you to take your temperature and then call the advice nurse. I heard you promise her that you would so I'm going to get you the thermometer, then I need to head back to work. Is there anything else you need before I go?"

"You know what else is weird?" Ethan asked, without answering Dan's question. "I would go back to Pescadero Creek right now. I mean, I can even taste it. Literally. My mouth tastes like wet earth and damp leaves, even earthworms."

"Yeah, I noticed that breath in the conference room," Dan said. He walked to the bathroom to find the thermometer. Ethan lay stiff and unmoving on top of the bed. He imagined he must look like an exhumed body. He could hear Dan fumbling in the bathroom, dropping things, as if his hands were trembling.

Ethan withdrew the thermometer from his mouth. As he moved it into view he glanced at the veins on the back of his hand, they were a deep red now. He stared at the thermometer, reading and re-reading it, trying to fathom its meaning. His body temperature was more than three degrees below normal now, yet the room was warm with summer heat. He lowered his hand to the crevice between the mattress and box spring and slid the thermometer in between, hiding it. He reached for the phone that Dan had left on the nightstand next to the bed. He found it hard to bend his elbows and even harder to straighten his fingers. It took several attempts before he could correctly dial the number for the advice nurse.

The staff at Dr. Adams' office seemed to be expecting Ethan's call. He was connected to the advice nurse and began to explain what had happened from the beginning. He described his passing out, his fatigue, and the strange degradation of body and mind. Yet, he regretted telling her anything, like he had something he needed to protect. After all, he had been remarkably healthy until yesterday. He hadn't been to the family doctor in over four years, even then the visit was for an injury. He began to doubt the need for the call.

The advice nurse was asking a lot of boiler-plate questions and Ethan was becoming agitated.

"Look, ma'am. I'm going to be fine. I only called because my wife asked me to. What I really need to do is sleep."

"I understand, Mr. Boyd."

If we can get a little more background information now it will help Dr. Adams in diagnosing you tomorrow. Do you mind if I ask you a couple more questions?"

Ethan stared at the ceiling above the bed. Everything in his field of vision had taken on a grainy appearance, and now it was as though the ceiling was made of sand, swarming and undulating above him.

"Hello? Mr. Boyd?"

"Oh, yeah. Sure. Go ahead."

"Have you traveled to any foreign countries, or have you been in contact with any untreated water?"

The question interrupted his increasingly torpid state. "If a stream is untreated water, then yes" he said. "My team from the office had completed more than half of the course and we were well ahead of the other teams. I had finished all the drinking water that I had in my bottle. We saw a creek on the map that ran parallel to the main trail that we were taking back to base camp. We made the detour and the guys cooled off in the shade while I filled my bottle and drank it down. Do you think that's what made me sick?"

"Well, you should never drink from unknown sources," said the nurse. We still don't have the results of your blood work but when the lab tests come back we'll know if it is Giardia or some other waterborne illness. Did you notice any foul odor to the water?"

"No, it was clear and delicious. We did notice something weird further upstream before we cut back to the main trail though."

"What was that?"

"About a hundred feet upstream we saw a dead rabbit at the water's edge"

"That doesn't sound good."

Ethan swallowed hard, his throat felt as though he was swallowing a fistful of leaves. A deep unrest came over him, then subsided. He started to recall more of what he had seen at the creek.

"It gets weirder," Ethan said. "While we were standing there looking at the rabbit, Dan, my friend from work, noticed a dead fox on the other side of the river. We were all staring at it, wondering what had happened, when all of the sudden it got up. It must have only been asleep, we figured. It was a pathetic little thing, forlorn and arthritic looking. It started pacing at the water's edge with its rigid little legs, growling and snapping at us. We just laughed and moved on."

"I think we're close to figuring out what is wrong with you, Mr. Boyd. The telling will be in the blood tests. We'll call you as soon as the results are back and Dr. Adams can go over everything with you when you see him tomorrow. To me it sounds like you picked up a nasty parasite or bacteria from the water you drank. Good thing is, it's very treatable if that is the case. You've done a good job listening to your body, rest will be the best thing for you now."

Ethan heard Audrey and the kids come home in the late afternoon. He felt like he was in a haze. He couldn't read the clock anymore but he heard them preparing dinner downstairs so he knew it must be after 5:00 pm. He could hear his wife's gentle voice explaining to Connor and Zoë that they had to be quiet because their daddy was not feeling well.

Ethan was drifting in and out of sleep but the line between the two had become more and more blurred. He kept having the same dream about waking up from under a writhing forest floor, life and death commingling under a blanket of rotting leaves. When Audrey tip-toed into the room he pretended to be asleep, his rigid hands and red veins hidden beneath the blankets. She gave him a kiss on the forehead and whispered, "Oh, Ethan. What is going on with you? You're like ice." She put another blanket on him and left the room.

He couldn't understand why he didn't want her help, anyone's help. In the hours since he first fell ill his concern had faded to nil. All that he knew to be normal was beginning to fade. The sounds of the outside world yielded to the slow dull thud of his heart, the spectrum of colors that his eyes afforded him were reduced to browns and muted reds. Still, he put up no fight against the changes and lay awake behind tired grey lids.

The phone rang and Ethan heard the answering machine on his dresser kick on after two rings. The machine beeped and a voice came on, "Hello, this is the advice nurse for Dr. Adams' office. This is a message for Ethan Boyd. Hello, is anybody there?"

Ethan threw off the leaden covers lying on top of him and swung his unbending legs to the floor. He didn't realize exactly how stiff he had become until he made his way across the room, throwing one leg in front of the other in a spastic motion.

The nurse continued speaking into the answering machine. "Mr. Boyd, I don't like leaving details on an answering machine but it is imperative that you get to a hospital as soon as possible. The blood tests came back and there are indications of a wide spread necrosis of the red blood cells. To put it simply, your blood is dying. We have never seen anything like …"

The voice went silent. Ethan lifted his finger from the 'Stop' button and pressed 'Delete'. He made his way slowly back to the bed. He pulled the covers on top of him in a tangled mess and lay back on the wet sheets, twisting them into balls between his clawed fingers.

The exertion of walking across the room made him feel tired, weighted, like he was sinking to the bottom of a murky pond, the room growing fainter as he sank deeper.

Later in the evening Ethan thought he heard his wife come in, straighten his covers, and whisper something about sleeping downstairs so she would not get sick as well. He wasn't sure if it was real or a dream.

He was so disconnected from the world he wasn't even sure if the room existed anymore.

In the isolating dark of night Ethan lay unmoving, each breath shallower than the last, each heartbeat fainter. The dawn came without him.

Dear wife, I am not Ethan anymore. I can see you sobbing over my cold body, my last breath hours ago. Yet I continue to live behind a filmy dead stare. My former self is all but gone, rapidly fading into a black void. Unnatural, unfamiliar impulses are all that remain. I can see only your rough outline through my idle, corrupted eyes. But I can smell you, wife, as you draw near to me, sense your living heartbeat. I have surrendered to a singular clarity, an eternal famine. My sulfurous teeth await your soft shoulder. Come closer so I may taste your life within my wooden mouth. My only existence now is to infect.

WAWONA

I lie in the back of my boyfriend Petey's truck, wet and cold, still in my new O'Neil wetsuit. I am unable to shiver, just as I am unable to do anything but stare. The tingling in my legs has spread to my arms and face. A voice speaks to me. A voice I haven't heard in years.

Where is he taking you, Maggie?
I don't know. Please let it be the hospital.

Petey has me gently wrapped in the woolen Mexican blanket that he pulled off the bench seat of his truck. It smells like beer and cigarettes, and even though the wind has engulfed the bed of his pick-up the smell lingers in my nostrils. Above the roar of the engine I can hear his voice coming from the cab of the truck, the same word over and over.

"Shit. Shit. Shit." The words punctuated by a fist to the dashboard.

I call to him. "Petey! Please stop. I need help." But these are only thoughts that are stuck somewhere in my head, thoughts that are unable to form into the words I need so desperately. The words I need to scream. The words that would stop the truck.

Red tiled roof tops go by in somber succession as we careen through the avenues. I roll side to side with each turn and pitch forward and backward at every stop sign but I remain on my back like a piece of driftwood, eyes fixed upon the darkening sky. The glow of the sunset has faded and a surreal metallic blue has begun to assume a position behind the clouds, their billowy outlines growing grayer at the edges. The wind lifts fronds of my wet hair, and I can taste the salt of the Pacific as they lick at my mouth and face.

Can you blink?
I'm not sure. Yes?

It was around three months ago, after my sixteenth birthday, that I first met Petey. Coming home from school one day I was surprised to find that they had moved my regular bus stop one block to the east for some reason, so I walked home a different way. I was nearing a house with tall hedges defining its property line and soon I could hear Led Zeppelin playing on a cheap portable radio. And then there was Petey, or P.D. Ziegler as I later learned. He was doing bench presses on a weight bench in his front yard.

The tall weeds that covered the yard were tickling his arms each time he brought the bar down, and he was alternating between laughing and grunting which made his Fu Manchu moustache look like two golden caterpillars racing down his face. He sat up and wiped his brow with his white tank top.

"You didn't see any cops down that way did you?" he asked. He extended his finger to point to the corner I had come from as he looked me up and down. Petey was the lovable screw up with the great body, directionless but so fun.

The streetlights pass over head, breaking up the darkening sky with their salmon glow. Suddenly the wind engulfing the bed of the truck starts to die. I slide forward as Petey downshifts into second gear and we begin to pull over. He stops the truck and jumps out without closing the door behind him. I hear his feet hurry up some stairs, and my heart sinks because I know there wouldn't be any stairs at the entrance of a hospital. "Oh Petey what are you doing? Please make the right decision."

I start to think that my older sister was right the whole time. "Petey is handsome, but not the sharpest tool in the shed," she would say. That's why I hid our relationship from everyone but her. Nobody would understand what a quiet honors student like me would see in such a reckless guy. But to me Petey is pure golden heat. Underneath the hard mantle is a warm loving core. With him I feel more alive than I knew was possible.

Now you feel cold?

Yes. So cold.

The sky is almost black now but the swirling metallic blue is spreading in the sky, getting bigger, brighter. I wonder if something is wrong, behind my eyes, inside my head. After a couple of minutes I hear the hurried shuffle of several feet coming down the stairs. I can hear voices getting closer until finally two faces come into view. They loom over me in the back of Petey's truck. Their shadowy outlines seem to marvel at the sight of me lying there, unmoving, like some mermaid hauled out of the ocean, now on display. As they move closer I can see that the faces belong to Devin O'Leary and

Tommy Breslin. Oh how I hate Tommy Breslin. They are smiling like it's Christmas morning and Devin says, "Is that Maggie Dunnigan? Dude, she is the finest chick at that all girl school, what's it called? Star of the Sea."

Petey appears over the back of the truck. His brow is furrowed and he lets out a long sigh. "Yeah, that's her," he says. He seems so worried and scared. I start to wonder what my injury is, what it looks like.

"Man, she looks hot," Tommy says between puffs of a cigarette.

The words make me cringe inside, but I know that my disgust will not be able to bubble to the surface. He takes a step away from the truck as Petey glares at him.

Devin moves in for a closer look. The smile erases from his face. "Dude, what's wrong with her?" he asks.

There is a long pause as Petey puts his hands over his face and pushes his golden mane back, locking his hands together behind his neck. Devin breaks the silence. "What the fuck happened, man?"

What did happen?

I'm not sure. But I am scared.

Petey grabs a cigarette from Tommy and begins to nervously clear his throat. I gaze straight up beyond their faces that glow orange with each drag of a cigarette, staring at the silent clouds that shift and morph like migrating leviathans.

"Well, we've been hanging out for a couple of months, you know taking it slow. Nobody really even knows we've been dating. The other day Maggie finds out my brother is Ronald Ziegler the surfer so she asks me if I can teach her how to surf."

"Shit," says Tommy. "You can't surf well enough to teach."

"Yeah, I know," says Petey. "But look at her. I can't say no to her. Nobody could."

I can see Petey studying Tommy with distrust. I know he doesn't like the way his best friend Devin has been spending more and more time with him. Tommy graduated from high school two years ago and he is a small-time drug dealer now. Petey spits contemptuously and continues his story. "So we pack up some boards after school and go down to Sloat. The waves were huge and sloppy and there were a lot of sleeper waves from the outside. But I couldn't let her down so we suited up. It took us almost thirty minutes to paddle out. She was exhausted and scared when we finally came up beyond the breakers. We didn't even have time to catch our breath before a fast moving set of outside waves came rolling in. We tried to paddle further out. Without warning, a twelve footer started breaking just as Maggie was trying to climb it. She went over the top and got pummeled. She was under for at least fifteen seconds."

"Oh man," says Devin. "Why can't she talk or move or anything?"

Petey didn't reply, instead he went on with the story. "I found her on shore with half of her broken board still tethered to her ankle by the leash. She was breathing and her eyes were open but she couldn't respond. I couldn't even tell if she was seeing me. She has this huge purple mark on her temple. Must've been from the tip of her board slamming into her head."

Petey lifts the blanket from the right side of my face and I hear gasps from Devin and Tommy.

Does it hurt?

No, I don't feel a thing.

Petey again swaddles me tightly in the rough blanket, then he gently strokes the side of my face with the back of his hand. I can't feel his touch, the warmth of his fingers. His fingers could always set me on fire, and now I worry I will never feel them, or anything else, again. I want to cry but I'm not sure I can even do that. Petey tells me it will be ok, that he will find me some help. "Petey please hurry. What are you waiting for?" I want to say.

I can see Devin leaning in to get a closer look at me. His face is all fear. "You have to take her to the hospital," he says.

"You know I can't do that," says Petey. "I'm supposed to be under house arrest. It will mean jail for me, man. You understand? Look, your sister is a nurse. Is she home? That is why I'm here. Can't she help us?"

"She's working until 11:00. And seriously, bro, I don't think you can wait."

Petey begins to punch and kick the truck. "Fuck," he yells. "What am I supposed to do? Devin, I need to use your phone. I need to call my brother."

Lying in the back of the truck, I see Devin and Petey disappear. The tingling now covers my whole body. I feel like I am living in a beehive with thousands of tiny wings beating against my skin. I can hear the ocean in my ears now too, like I have a seashell held to each. The spreading numbness is soothing. I feel like I could just float away into its soft whiteness.

Are you dying?

Do you think I am?

The momentary calm is immediately erased as Tommy peers over the bed of the truck again. I didn't realize that he had not gone upstairs with Petey and Devin. His eyes look like they are just shadows under his pronounced forehead. Even in the dark I can see his pockmarked skin. "Hi beautiful," he says.

Tommy puts his cigarette out on the side of the truck and then reaches in and starts to peel away the blanket Petey has me so carefully wrapped in. He starts roughly combing his fingers through my hair, and then he lifts my head slightly. I realize that he is trying to get at the zipper of my wetsuit. His face turns angry as he struggles to find the top of the zipper. I want to yell for Petey, but instead I continue to lie motionless, my cold body not responding to my commands.

I hear the zipper begin to unzip and Tommy moves both hands under my wetsuit. I can see that his hands are now on my chest. I would spit in his face if I could. Spit in his eye. He turns his head to meet my gaze and says, "I knew they would be nice".

I hear footsteps again but Tommy doesn't, he is too caught up in fondling me. In a blur of flesh and flannel Petey's fist collides with his jaw. I can hear the snap of bone. Tommy's hands almost seem to wave goodbye as they follow his body to the pavement. Muffled thuds come from the sidewalk next to the truck. It sounds like someone is puffing up a large pillow, and I realize that

Petey is kicking Tommy as he lies on the ground. "What the fuck are you doing?" asks Devin on the run. He slams Petey against the truck and it sways like a raft caught in a ship's wake.

Petey has his back to me. He runs his right hand through his hair and I can see that it is bloody. Devin glances at my open wetsuit as he holds Petey against the rear fender. "Were you trying to kill him?" Devin asks. "Don't you think that might land you in jail, dumb ass? My sister isn't home, your brother didn't answer the phone, and Maggie's hurt. What are you going to do, Petey?"

Petey pushes Devin off of him and sighs. Holding his head down, Petey shields his eyes like he has a headache. "You're right man," he says. "I just lost it. I'm losing my fucking mind. But that scumbag had it coming, Dev." He walks over to him, puts his hand on his back and mumbles something. I can see them lift up Tommy and they walk away from my view.

A moment later Petey returns. Leaning over the truck he looks me in the eye and whispers, "sorry". He begins to zip up my wetsuit and I can see tears starting to well up in his brown eyes. His face is hovering over mine and a tear falls from his eye. I think it hit my cheek but I can't feel it. I start to cry. I see Petey's left hand gently brush my face and he wipes a tear away, maybe it was his own. He whispers how beautiful he thinks I am and how everything will be ok.

I can see now in the sky above him that the evening fog is moving in. It is carrying the smell of the Pacific, salty and alive. The blue glow is now swirling and iridescent, like one of the nebulas I learned about in Mrs. Merkel's science class. Petey disappears from view and I hear the truck door slam. The engine starts and we drive off into the thick fog that is now creeping into every corner of neighborhood.

Do you like the fog?

No, but I like the way it makes everything quiet.

Petey is driving more slowly now. I don't know how many minutes have passed since we left Devin's house. Time has ceased to exist for me. I drift deeper into isolation. The droning engine, the creaking of the truck bed, the radio; all have yielded to the sound of the ocean in my head. The waves become louder with every passing block.

The smell of eucalyptus suddenly cuts through the fog. I breathe in its incense and the familiarity is calming. I am so tired I just don't care where we are going anymore. I only want to sleep. We pass under a lavender balloon tangled in the telephone wires above. It has pink letters that say Happy Birthday. I wonder if it might be one of the balloons from little Mary Macready's birthday party last week. She lives down the street from me. Maybe Petey is taking me home.

It is as if the truck is now floating in the fog. We drift so slowly I can read a street sign as we pass. Wawona. The street my house is on, the street where I have lived all my life. The sound of the surf is so loud now. It is almost all that I am. My body feels like it is made from ice and yet I am not bothered by it.

Can you come with me now?

Yes.

The swirling mass of fog lifts me from the back of Petey's truck. I begin to rise up over the truck and slowly roll over, suspended in the bluish white cloud. It is all like a dream. I look down and see droplets of saltwater falling from me into the truck below as I float further upward. I hover above it like a kite. We are slowly inching our way down my street.

Wawona is an Indian name. It's also the name I gave my imaginary friend when I was a little girl. I would talk to her when I was lonely or sad, or when my parents were fighting. My mom said I outgrew her when I was around six years old, but today she is back. We hold hands and look at all the familiar houses together as we glide down the street. I am no longer scared.

Do you remember this house?

Yes of course. My mom left me with Mrs. Boyle every day on her way to work. Her kids used to scrape the old chewing gum off the sidewalks with their teeth and then chew it all day.

Gross.

Totally.

What was the name of the older boy who used to live in this house? The one who buried you up to your neck in his backyard?

Tommy Breslin.

That's right. What a creep. The lady in this pink house used to give you and your friends ice cream right?

Yes. That is until I tried out some swear words I had just learned instead of saying thank you.

You got a bad spanking after that.

I remember we talked a lot that day.

Looks like Petey is pulling up in front of your house now. You're home now.

Thank you, Wawona. When I was a little girl you were always there for me, my special friend. My secret friend. Goodbye.

Bye.

Petey opens the tailgate and carefully pulls me from back of his truck. I am like a rag doll in his arms as he carries me up the terrazzo steps to my front door. I am so tired I feel as though there is no blood left in my veins. He lays me down on the landing and I stare into his sad eyes. They have the look of complete devastation and sadness. He wraps me tighter in the wool blanket, kisses me on the forehead, then the lips. I can taste the salt of his tears, the salt of ocean.

Petey slowly turns to descend the stairs, no knock at the door, no push of the doorbell. I watch him disappear from view into the recess of cowardice as the fog engulfs me entirely. Directly above my skyward gaze I can see Wawona again. *Wait*, is all she says, and then she is gone. From inside the house I can hear my father's voice coming to the door. "Did you hear something?" he says.

THE ABSCONDING SEA

The man stood at the end of the pier, toes to the edge, family dog by his side. He gazed out to the harbor, searching, as he had for the last several evenings, for direction. Elliot Smith didn't know from where this direction would come, or where it would take him for that matter, but he looked for it at every opportunity. He watched the sailboats bobbing peacefully against the setting sun. Their latent agility was exactly what he wanted for his own life, to be able to change course with minimal opposition.

The voluptuous August air made him feel momentarily younger than the autumn that had settled into his core. He watched the last slice of sun, just shy of crimson, like a wedge of blood orange, sink into the Nantucket Sound. The sky held onto the muted afterglow for several minutes, like flush upon a lover's skin. Then the pier lights came on as the evening sky cooled to a dusky azure. Elliot knew then it was time to return to the musty cottage he had rented for his family, but he was never in a hurry to get back to the airless bungalow, the bickering, the spoiled children.

He took in a deep breath as if it would be his last for the evening. Holding his flip-flops in one hand he let his bare toes caress the worn wood planking of the pier, made smooth by decades of vacationing feet. Finally he turned to find his dog, Gus, and in doing so stepped squarely onto his tail. It felt like a writhing snake under his foot and Gus let out a yowl that sent Elliot off balance. He waved his arms like twin windmills, but his weight had already shifted too far. He began to fall off the pier.

As Elliot was falling, before he hit his head on a 14' sloop, his biggest concern was the fate of his cell phone. The thud of his head striking against the boat, followed by a sizable splash, went unnoticed by anyone else milling about the pier, and Elliot's limp body drifted slowly downward, like a leaf falling from the sky. He settled on the sandy bottom like a dying fish. Perhaps his unconscious mind sensed he was underwater because he didn't take a breath right away. He just lay there; face up under twelve feet of water.

After a few seconds he regained consciousness and, of course, attempted to breathe. He caught his mistake immediately and was able to stop the intrusion of water in his throat, pushing it back out with his remaining breath. The blow to his head had imparted a temporary befuddlement, but looking up he could see the outline of Gus peering over the edge of the dock, barking furiously. The water that surrounded Elliot had an ethereal quality, shimmering and iridescent under the yellow light from the pier. It was like being suspended in gold dust. He started to swim to surface and cut through the water with a determined breaststroke.

Almost instantly he felt something tighten around his left ankle, preventing him from reaching the surface. He reached down and could feel that he had somehow become entangled in a rope. It was coiled around his ankle and felt taut, like it was anchored to something heavy, maybe even the pier itself. His ascension had made the rope tighter, rescinding the promise of air.

Elliot began to panic. He fumbled at the rope with desperate fingers, getting nowhere. Too much time had elapsed and his lungs started convulsing, begging for oxygen.

As he struggled with the rope he thought he saw something moving toward him. It looked like a woman. A naked woman. Her lean form cut through the water effortlessly, and in an instant she was upon him, staring at him with curious blue-green eyes. He didn't know where she came from but he didn't care either.

His lungs ached and a strange tingling was beginning to overtake his body. Elliot knew that soon, very soon, his lungs would win the battle with his brain and he would breathe in water and die. He frantically gestured to his tethered leg, but the woman swam off as if frightened.

The introduction of hope and its unexpected departure eroded his ability to stave off the inevitable and he could feel the briny water working its way between his quivering lips. Suddenly he felt a tug at his leg. He looked down to find that the woman had not swum off. She was under him, her slender fingers deftly unknotting the rope.

The tingling yielded to a creeping numbness and he began to take in water. His freedom came too late. He was sliding through unconsciousness clear to the other side—when suddenly he became aware of his lungs filling with warm sweet air. A velvety breath was pushing life back into him, displacing the water that had found its way in. It was intoxicating, unlike anything he had known.

Elliot opened his eyes and could see her face in front of his, her hands gently cradling his head. He could feel her full lips pressed against his and the slight touch of her tongue upon his own. She withdrew and through the filtered twilight of the Atlantic he marveled at her transcendent beauty. Her long hair danced toward him in the water, the tips lightly touching his face. Her breath was like a drug. It was as if time had stopped. He felt no need to hurry to the surface, to the life he had built on land.

The woman took his hands in hers and looked at him with the curiosity of a child. Her lips drew into a subtle smile and she started to pull him through the water toward the shore. Her graceful undulations propelled him with astonishing speed, and he wondered if she were an off-duty lifeguard.

She ran him aground and he rolled over, breathing in the heavy New England air in deep gasps. He was sad to let go of her breath, but her spell remained. He never felt more alive. She moved on top of him, pushing herself up with her hands upon his chest. Under the moonlight she was even more rarefied. Her wet hair clung to her skin like fronds of seaweed, partially obscuring her small breasts. Elliot couldn't believe any of it was happening.

She leaned in and gave him a kiss, her tongue carrying the salt of the sea, alive and life-giving. He put his arms around her and pulled her close, but she wriggled free and spun around, plunging back into the water. He sat up to watch her under the light of the moon, feeling no surprise as he watched the tail of a large fish disappear into the sea.

"Because your father is crazy," said Michelle, Elliot's wife.

Emma, their youngest child, twisted her face into a pout. "But when will Daddy come home, Mommy?" she asked.

"Why don't you ask him, honey?"

Elliot stood at the window of the rented cottage, holding his eye to the cheap telescope he had just bought, scanning the ocean.

"Daddy, why aren't you coming home with us?"

Elliot could hear their voices but he wasn't listening. It had been a week since he fell off the pier and a new insatiable hunger had settled into him. His thoughts were only of the woman and the sea. He completely forgot that school would start in two days.

Emma sidled up to him, tugging on his Nantucket red shorts. She asked him again, "Daddy, how come you aren't coming home with us?"

"What? Oh. Well baby, Daddy has some important work to do." He squatted down and gently held her skinny arms. "When he finishes his work he'll come straight home." He smiled a cursory smile, then gave her a kiss on the forehead and returned to the scope.

His wife laughed sardonically, her voice hoarse from days of fighting with him behind closed doors. She pinched the laugh off midway and in a flat tone addressed their daughter. "Go on down to the car, honey," she said. "Your brother is waiting in the backseat. Mommy needs to talk to Daddy."

Emma reluctantly obeyed. She stepped onto the weathered porch and turned to look at her father one last time. "Go," her mother commanded, and she scampered down the stairs. Elliot didn't even notice that she had left the room. His eye was glued to the telescope, combing the shore for any sign of the woman from the sea. He felt as though he was going through some sort of withdrawal and only she could make him whole again.

Michelle got up from the breakfast table, accidentally kicking over the empty wine bottle she had left on the floor the night before. She walked with charged steps to the living room and stood opposite her husband.

"I don't know what the hell is wrong with you," she said. "Ever since you fell off the pier you have been acting strange. You spend all your time in the ocean or just sitting on the beach, staring out to the water. You haven't interacted with me or the kids for days. What is it you're looking for? Tell me, damn it."

Elliot stepped away from the scope and sighed, not because he felt compelled to explain himself again, but because he felt his desperate searching would continue to go unrewarded.

"Michelle, I've told you. I don't know what is happening to me. All I know is when I came out of that water, I came out a different man. I can't explain. It's almost like I died and was reborn, given a new life. You know?"

"No, I don't"

"It's like I've formed some sort of bond."

"Bond with what?"

Elliot hesitated before answering. "The sea," he said.

"Oh my God, are you serious?"

He walked back to the window and stared at the grey-blue water. "Yes, I am," he said.

"You are an idiot, Elliot. A deluded, self-centered idiot. Don't you care at all about your family? What am I supposed to tell the kids?"

"I just need to be near the ocean a little longer. That's all I'm asking for."

Michelle walked over to the fireplace, unable to look at him any longer. She was mindlessly examining the shell covered picture frames upon the mantle.

"What about your job?" she said, still facing the fireplace. "Have you thought about that? You'll lose your job at the paper, you know that?

Elliot shuttered, repulsed by the thought of being bound to his mid-town office, walled off from the sea. He returned to his telescope. "Screw them. They were going to make me a blogger anyway."

Michelle turned, her voice trembling. "You've really lost your mind, do you know that?" She began to cry.

Elliot still loved his wife but something had crept into him, making him singularly focused. Still, at least for the moment, he felt bad for what he was putting his family through. He stopped his search and made an attempt at consoling her. "Come on Shell, don't cry. Remember when you said 'life is a journey'?"

Michelle stopped crying. "Abandoning your family is a journey?" She grabbed her keys from the table. "Fuck you," she said as she walked past him, slamming the door to the cottage on the way out. The walls shook from the force and a painting of a tall ship fell to the floor. He winced at the crash and then walked slowly over to the painting. He picked up the broken frame and looked at the vessel depicted within.

Elliot could feel the hairs on his arms rise as he stared at the illustration. On the prow of the ship was the figure of a woman. She bore a remarkably close resemblance to the woman who saved his life. The name of the ship was displayed on its bow and he smiled wryly as he read it, *The Destiny*.

It had been over a week since Michelle left with the children and Elliot's desperation grew. The ocean called to him day and night. He spent his days swimming its depths until his muscles ached, looking for her, the woman from the sea. She had breathed new life into him but now he began to feel as though she had taken something too. It was though he was being consumed. He lost his appetite and grew lean and hard. The vitality she had given him was being replaced by a profound ache, an unyielding desire to be with her. His nerves felt raw and exposed.

Long hours were spent in the water, searching. As the sun would go down he would sit on shore at the water's edge, casting a long solitary shadow upon the wind blown sand. He slept less and ate very little.

Nearly three weeks after his fall Elliot did lose his job. The news came to him by way of one of the many berating voicemails Michelle left for him. He had also learned that she transferred all of the funds from their joint accounts to her private checking account. This left him with access to very little money. He couldn't blame her for being angry. As he threw his replacement phone off the end of the pier, he knew she was right, he had gone mad.

No longer able to afford the cottage he rented with his family, Elliot was forced to downsize. He was lucky enough to secure a one room shack near the end of a point, which was ideal for his tireless seeking. It was an artist's studio, built in the 1800s, with no electricity or heat, only the basic comforts. It was meant to be a day-use retreat—the property owner actually asked him what kind of art he would be making in the studio—so the next day Elliot showed him the shell frames from the cottage the family had rented. He knew he could maintain a constant vigil from the shack and would do anything to secure the lease.

The days stretched into weeks and Elliot settled into a hermitic lifestyle. His beard grew long and he became a powerful swimmer. He taught himself to catch fish using a tattered fishing net that he found on the shore one day. He cooked his simple meals over driftwood fires, all the while casting one eye to the water.

The ocean became the only place he felt comfortable. While enveloped in its salty embrace he could feel the tremble of a connection, knowing that somewhere within its fluid expanse she was swimming with a grace worthy of legend. He wondered if soon he would become more like her, but the transformation he waited for never came, only more hunger.

Toward the end of summer a tropical storm formed, bringing fierce winds and torrential rain. High waves and a surging tide forced Elliot to retreat to his meager cottage. The winds bayed at his door and rattled the windows, filling the room with an unsettling wooden chatter. The rafters creaked and moaned like the timbers of a ship. The sounds were almost mammalian. Elliot felt like he was holed up in the belly of a dying beast. Water found its way in through unseen holes in the roof and soon it was as if the whole cottage was crying. Elliot looked out through the filmy window panes and could see that the waves had become very large. When they broke, the whitewater came all the way to his door.

He stood at the window for hours, unmoving like a sentinel at his post, watching. A cottony dryness pervaded his mouth and he stepped away from the window to get a drink of water. When he turned he thought he saw something move in the small antique mirror that hung on the otherwise unadorned pine walls. He slowly walked over to the mirror, his back to the wall as he approached, as though he needed the element of surprise.

When he turned to face the mirror he froze, seeing not his own reflection but her face. The woman from the sea. It was as if she were floating behind the glass in turbid green water. The water looked as though it were illuminated, and she beckoned him nearer, pulling him closer with her eyes, they themselves limpid avatars of the living ocean. Elliot wondered if he was going mad, but his visceral reaction convinced him otherwise. The force of her pull was impossible to resist, and he hungered for the spirit within her lips, to be made whole again. He closed his eyes and drew close to kiss her parted lips through the glass.

Outside thunder cracked the sky and the cottage trembled in its wake. Elliot opened his eyes and recoiled upon seeing his own face. It was haggard and drawn, ghoulishly white in the lightning filled room. He stumbled backward until he hit the wall behind him. He slid down to the floor and began to hyperventilate. He brought his shaking hands to his face and wondered if the line separating fantasy from reality had become permanently blurred.

He could hear waves lapping at the edge of the porch. The ocean was slowly creeping under the door and he could smell its ancient infinity. Suddenly he heard what sounded like knocking at the door. He quickly dismissed it as a piece of driftwood that was carried in by the waves, but then he saw the doorknob turn from side to side.

Elliot bolted up from the floor and lunged for the door, ready to stare into the mouth of madness. He swung it open and was met by pelting rain driven by gale force winds. It was all he could do to keep his eyes open. Sea foam writhed against the perimeter of the cottage and he could see a huge wave retreating back into the ocean. It was then that he saw her, cutting through the chop, her movements empyreal, even amongst the violence of an enraged sea.

Elliot ran into the ocean. He called out to her, trying to be heard above the storm. He swam hard and fast in her direction, slashing through the heavy sea. He pushed onward, determined and possessed, until he saw her lithesome body disappear into the grey Atlantic, propelling her streamline body through the chop with economy and grace. He thought he saw her tail wave in the air as she dove down to the deeper waters of home. The pounding waves and wind escorted Elliot back to land, and he lay face down on the shore, like a dead man.

The cool chill of autumn snaps at his ankles as he sits on the desolate beach. Elliot stares at the ocean with hollow eyes, peering out from behind bended knees, pulled tight to his chest for warmth. He sits alone, the only evidence of human life. All have ridden out on the tail of summer, back to their homes, jobs, families. Elliot, now gaunt and expended, has resigned to never leave the shore. He no longer cares for food or shelter, only the dream of her warm breath, filling his lungs and returning his soul.

CPSIA information can be obtained at www.ICGtesting.com
Printed in the USA
BVOW030213250613

324225BV00001B/3/P